"If you were ... same thing. We ... help us? All we want is to find out how our friend died," I said.

"You should have told me that in the first place," the man answered. "I'm a believer in truth, justice, and the American way—just like Superman." He handed me the box. "I just don't like to be pushed around."

He turned and headed deeper into the subway.

"Where's he going?" Joe whispered. "The Batcave?"

"Wrong superhero," I answered. "Wherever he's going, I don't . . ."

The words evaporated in my mouth. My suddenly dry mouth. The air around me was . . . vibrating. Then the ground started to shake.

Two small circles of blinding light appeared in the darkness.

"Train!" yelled Joe.

THE HARDY BOYS
UNDERCOVER BROTHERS®

Available from Simon & Schuster

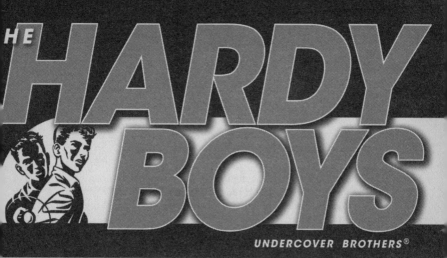

THE HARDY BOYS

UNDERCOVER BROTHERS®

#18   Pushed

FRANKLIN W. DIXON

Aladdin Paperbacks

New York   London   Toronto   Sydney

This book is a work of fiction. Any references to historical events, real people, or real locales are used fictitiously. Other names, characters, places, and incidents are the product of the author's imagination, and any resemblance to actual events or locales or persons, living or dead, is entirely coincidental.

❧ ALADDIN PAPERBACKS
An imprint of Simon & Schuster Children's Publishing Division
1230 Avenue of the Americas, New York, NY 10020
Copyright © 2007 by Simon & Schuster, Inc.
All rights reserved, including the right of reproduction in whole or in part in any form.
THE HARDY BOYS MYSTERY STORIES and HARDY BOYS UNDER-COVER BROTHERS are registered trademarks of Simon & Schuster, Inc.
ALADDIN PAPERBACKS and related logo are registered trademarks of Simon & Schuster, Inc.
Designed by Lisa Vega
The text of this book was set in Aldine 401 BT.
Manufactured in the United States of America
First Aladdin Paperbacks edition September 2007
10 9 8 7 6 5 4 3
Library of Congress Control Number 2007921471
ISBN-13: 978-1-4169-4802-5
ISBN-10: 1-4169-4802-3

TABLE OF CONTENTS

1.
POISONED PILOT

"We shut that place *down*," Joe said. He glanced out the window of the Cessna Skylane and watched the Miller Academy grow smaller and smaller as we flew away.

I swallowed hard. "Yeah. And it needed it. It was like a school for hate crimes." I pushed the throttle forward. I wanted to get a little more altitude.

"You're sweating like a hog," Joe told me.

"I know." I used the bottom of my shirt to wipe off my face.

"It's Dr. Miller who should be sweating. He's never going to teach again. Forget about treating patients," Joe said.

I swallowed again. "Yeah. Using his psychiatric training to make the students at his school violent—

1

that was seriously evil." Parents usually sent a kid to Miller after they'd been booted from at least one other school. Dr. Miller, the head of the academy, had a reputation for being able to get any kid—no matter how "troubled"—straightened out.

And maybe there was a time when he was even good at it. Then he got fascinated by what caused violent behavior and started doing experiments with the kids at his school. He didn't stop even when one of his human lab rats got violent enough to seriously injure a teacher.

I had to swallow again.

"You want a soda?" Joe asked. "We don't have anything cold, but we have a couple cans left over from when we flew in."

"Better not," I said. I ran one hand through my hair. Sweat had it plastered to my head. "I'm already dying to go to the bathroom."

Joe clucked. "What would Aunt Trudy say? You're always supposed to go before you leave home, even if you're just going to be gone for ten minutes."

I laughed, and a little saliva spilled out of my mouth. I wiped it off with my sleeve.

Joe stared at me. "Like you're not a total slob," I told him.

"SLUDGE," said Joe, eyes wide.

"Sludge?" I repeated.

"Salivation, lacrimation, urination, diarrhea, gastric upset, and emesis," Joe rattled off. "Remember from the ATAC first-aid class? I think Miller fed us poisonous mushrooms in that salad. Frank, you have muscarine poisoning."

"You're not showing any symptoms," I pointed out. "And you ate the salad too."

"I hate mushrooms, remember? I picked mine out." Joe dug around in his pocket and pulled out a handful of mushroom pieces. "I stashed them when Miller wasn't looking. I didn't want to be rude to the demented criminal. Aunt Trudy believes there's no excuse for bad table manners."

He reached over and put his fingers on the side of my neck. "Your pulse is up," he told me after about fifteen seconds.

"Wait, am I crying?" I asked.

"Yeah, that's lacrimation," Joe informed me. "We've got to get you to a hospital. Are you going to be able to keep flying this thing?"

I looked at the instrument panel. It was a blur of red and white. "My vision's affected now. You better take over."

"Just keep her straight for one minute while I find a place for an emergency landing. We need to get you to a doctor, now." Joe pulled out our map.

I squinted, bringing the dials back into focus.

"Okay, there's a hospital about seventy miles from here," my brother said. "The map shows a nice, big patch of green behind it. There are a lot of potato fields around here. I'm betting it's one of them. We can do an emergency landing. Let's trade places. I'll slide over, you slide under."

My stomach turned over, and the nausea made my head spin.

"Come on, Frank. Move," Joe urged.

"I don't think I can," I admitted.

Joe leaned across me and nudged the yoke to the left. "We need to head ten degrees west. That should do it. Just hold it steady for another sec while I radio for help."

I nodded, swallowing down the saliva that kept flooding my mouth. I flicked the perspiration and tears away from my eyes, but I still couldn't see the dial of the compass. So I just followed Joe's instructions and held the yoke as firmly as I could with my sweat-slick hands.

"Okay, an ambulance is going to meet us. The field is coming up. You see it?" asked Joe.

"I see it," I told him. "And I hope my eyesight is getting worse. Those aren't trees in the potato field, are they?"

"I guess I was wrong about the potato part," Joe

admitted. "But those trees are about a mile out. That gives us enough space to land." He leaned over and took the yoke again.

"Just barely," I commented.

"Just barely is more than enough for me," Joe answered. "Get the field lined up with your right wing tip," he muttered, coaching himself. "Altimeter should be at one thousand."

My stomach gave another flip-flop. *Symptom, not fear,* I thought.

"Okay, we're going in. Hang on." Joe pulled back on the throttle to slow us down.

"Careful not to let the nose drop too far," I warned.

"You worry about the rudder pedals," Joe shot back as he released the landing gear. "I can't reach them from over here." He pulled all the way back on the throttle, then brought the yoke back a little.

We hit the bumpy ground hard—and bounced. We hit again and stayed there, tearing across the long grass.

"Trees," Joe reminded me.

I blinked rapidly to clear my vision. Yep, there were trees. And we were going to crash into them. We were going way too fast to avoid it.

I used the rudder pedals to position the body of

the plane between the two trees that looked far-thest apart. A little left. Too far. A tiny bit right. This was it. There was no time for anything else.

My body jerked as the plane slammed into the trees. But I'd gotten us lined up so the wings took most of the impact.

"You okay?" I asked my brother.

"Excellent tree crashing! You did it!" he cried over the wail of the approaching ambulance.

"I did it. And now I think I need to vomit," I told him.

2.
PUSHED?

"Aunt Trudy, Frank wants oyster dressing this year."

I couldn't resist tormenting my brother. I pulled a jar of the slimies off the supermarket shelf and waved them in front of Frank. His face went as gray as the crustaceans—just like it had before he puked all over the instrument panel of the plane. Wait, make that mollusks. Crustaceans are the ones with the flexible carapaces, not shells. See, I'm as much of a science guy as Frank. Yet I am cooler and better at video games.

"Frank Hardy, you always rave about how much you love my chestnut stuffing," Aunt T scolded. "Are you telling me you'd rather have oyster?"

"No!" Frank said quickly. He shoved the oysters

out of his sight line and glared at me. I gave a snort of laughter. I know, I know. The oyster thing was totally juvenile. But I had to give Frank a little extra torment—just to show I was glad he was still alive.

"Are you sure?" Aunt Trudy pressed. "It's your Thanksgiving. I want you to have your favorites. I can make oyster and chestnut."

"No, really, thanks, Aunt Trudy, but I'm not hungry," answered Frank.

Aunt Trudy laughed. "Thanksgiving isn't for almost two weeks," she reminded him. "I hope you'll find your appetite by then."

"I may never eat again," Frank mumbled.

Aunt Trudy didn't hear him. She'd taken off down the aisle, racing a woman toward the last turkey-shaped cake pan. Aunt T won. I knew she would. She's sort of old. But she's fast—and crafty.

Actually, she'd make a great ATAC agent, except for the part where the *T* stands for "Teens." The American Teens Against Crime organization was set up by Frank's and my father. Dad figured there were some situations—situations like your basic mad scientist trying to make reform school kids more vicious—where teens were the best possible operatives because they could fit in in a way that adults couldn't. He's a retired cop, so he knows all about infiltration, and going undercover, and the rest of that covert stuff. He isn't crazy about me and Frank getting in dangerous situations—he's a dad, after all—but he knows that we're helping put away the bad guys, and that makes him proud.

Aunt Trudy and Mom would be proud of us too—after they finished killing us for risking our necks. So it's probably better that they don't know.

"You're going to make your giblet gravy again this year, aren't you, Aunt T?" I asked. Because Frank's face had gotten pretty much back to normal color, and I wanted to see if I could make it go green this time.

"Of course. I'm famous for it," Aunt Trudy answered.

"What are giblets again?" I scratched my head, like I was trying to think. Okay, sometimes I carry things to far.

"Heart, liver, gizzard," Aunt Trudy listed off. "I chop them up kind of coarse, and—"

"We need cereal," Frank burst out. He hadn't gone green exactly, but his face definitely wasn't any of the healthy human colors. "I'll go get it."

And he was outta there.

I laughed. I couldn't help it. I'm a fun-loving kind of guy. A crackling sound came over the grocery store audio system, and I thought I might hear a "clean up in aisle" whatever aisle the cereal was on. Instead I heard my own name.

"Joe Hardy, you have won the Gobble Gobble Goodies Prize of the Day. Come on down to cash register three to pick it up," a girl called over the intercom.

"Go see what you won, Joe!" cried Aunt Trudy. "I hope it's the biggest turkey in the place."

I headed toward the front of the store. I suspected Frank had figured out a way to get me back for trying to make him puke. Aunt Trudy isn't the only crafty one in the family.

"I'm Joe Hardy," I said when I reached register three.

"Then Theresa is yours," the checker told me.

"I'm hoping your name is Theresa," I replied. She was really cute, with her blond hair all scooped up on the top of her head.

"Uh, no, it's not," the girl answered. She pointed to her name tag. I hadn't noticed it before. It read JULIANNA in big red letters.

"My brother isn't that observant," said Frank as he stepped up behind me.

Julianna smiled at him, in that flirty way 98 percent of girls smile at my brother. The sad thing is, he usually doesn't notice. And when he does, he blushes.

FRANK

Frank here. I don't think all this discussion about the various colors my face can turn adds anything to the—

JOE

Joe here. And I'm telling this part of the story. Take your face and the rest of you on out of here.

So anyway, suddenly Julianna was shoving this huge turkey piñata into my arms. It was crazy-looking. Its feathers were bright pink and it had eyelashes about a foot long. "*This* is Theresa," Julianna explained. "I think you two make an adorable couple."

"I do too," Frank added.

"I didn't actually enter a contest or anything." I shifted Theresa so that her beak wasn't about to peck my eye out—and that's when I heard it. A muffled thunking sound. There was something inside my turkey, and I didn't think it was candy. Or giblets. "But thanks," I added quickly. I rushed out to the parking lot, Frank on my heels.

"Aunt Trudy still needs help with those two

11

carts of groceries," he reminded me.

"I know. Just give me one second." I shoved my hand into the turkey and felt a game cassette inside. I was right. "We've got a mission," I told Frank.

Frank and I helped unload and stow the mountain of food Aunt Trudy thought was necessary for our family Thanksgiving. Then we headed up to his room. We quickly emptied out the turkey piñata and ended up with the game cartridge labeled "Runaway," a map of the New York City Subway, and two plane tickets to LaGuardia Airport.

"We've got a sweet New York City mission," I said, holding up the tickets.

"Let's see just how sweet," answered Frank. He slid the game cassette into the player.

A video began to play. My eyes flicked back and forth as I tried to take in everything at once. The video showed a subway station—an NYC Subway station, I assumed. Yellow crime-scene tape was strung between the cement pillars that ran down the station, blocking access to the edge of the platform.

"I don't like this already," Frank said, his eyes on the cop who had just ducked under the tape line. He handed an empty vinyl body bag down to someone on the tracks.

The image faded and was replaced by some

grainy black-and-white footage of a crowded city street. A yellow arrow pointed at a teenage guy in grubby clothes carrying a cardboard box.

"Evan Davis. Age fifteen," the low, serious voice of our ATAC contact began. *"This footage was taken by an electronics store security camera approximately five minutes before he entered the Astor Place subway station. Ten minutes later he was dead, hit by a subway train. It is unclear if his death was an accident . . . or murder."*

A new image appeared—a color photo of Evan and a couple of other teenagers in front of a four-story building of gray stone. A sky blue sign with yellow daisies on it read THE HAVEN.

"Davis ran away from his home in Lake Ronkonkoma, New York, two months before his death. For the six weeks before he died, he was staying at the Haven, a center for runaway teens at five-seventeen, West Twenty-third Street in Manhattan."

I couldn't take my eyes off Evan's face as our contact continued to give us the deets.

"Davis was scheduled to meet Gwen Anderson, a reporter with the Village Voice, *on the day he was killed. Anderson claims that Davis wanted to talk to her about what he described as 'something bad' that was going on at the Haven. That's all he would tell Anderson over the phone. She says he sounded agitated and frightened the day he made the appointment with her."*

A new photo came up: a series of items tagged as evidence—a beat-up wallet, a small pocket knife, a piece of paper with Gwen Anderson's number on it.

"Nothing in Davis's possession indicated what he intended to tell the reporter," our contact went on.

A film clip began to run, a commercial about the Haven and all the kids the center helped. The clip showed teenagers playing basketball, doing homework together at a big table, having a food fight with big smiles on their faces. Then it flashed to the same kids sleeping on the streets, begging for money, eating food from a trash can. The commercial ended with a plea for charitable contributions.

I could totally see my parents sending in money after watching it. The Haven looked like a good place—a safe place.

"Your mission is to go undercover at the Haven," our contact said. *"Davis thought there was something criminal happening at the center. Find out what it is. And, most importantly, find out if Davis was pushed off that subway platform."*

3.
RUNAWAYS

Joe and I stared at the blank screen of the game player as the cartridge destroyed itself. The cartridges always self-destruct as part of ATAC's security system.

"That was . . ." Joe let his words trail off.

"Yeah," I answered. The two of us have worked on cases involving death before, but thinking about Evan Davis getting run over by the train—that was gut-wrenching. Had someone pushed him? Was someone responsible? Or had Evan just fallen?

"What do you think Evan could have known that would make somebody willing to kill him like that?" Joe asked.

"If it was a murder," I said.

Joe raised one eyebrow, a skill he'd practiced in

15

the mirror for more than a month until he got it down. "Pretty big coincidence that it happened when he was on his way to give a reporter the scoop on the badness going on at the Haven."

"True," I agreed. "But we still shouldn't go into the case with assumptions in place."

"So what do you think he found out about the center? Could it be a cult, you think? Or maybe they use the kids for organ donors. Or maybe—"

"Organ donors?" I protested.

"Yeah. Haven't you heard that story? The one about this guy who woke up in a hotel room after the junior prom with one of his kidneys gone," Joe answered.

"Oh, right. Yeah, it's definitely either organ harvesting, or Evan found out there were alligators in the toilets of the Haven," I told him.

"Wait. I'm supposed to be the sarcastic one," Joe shot back. "And organs go for big money."

"I'll give you that," I agreed. "But I think it's pointless to try to guess what's going on at the Haven until we get there and have at least a little intel."

Joe flopped back on his lumpy bed. Lumpy because Joe makes it by just tossing the bedspread over the tangle of sheets and blankets. "So what's our cover story? Why did we run away? What's our deal?"

I sat down in front of Joe's computer and googled "why teens run away." I clicked on the top link. "Wow. This website says forty percent of kids who run away have been locked out of the house. They're called throwaways."

Joe's eyes widened, then he grinned. "Aunt Trudy locked us out of the house once. Remember? We decided to make mudpies in the kitchen."

"She locked us out in our own backyard for about three minutes," I reminded him.

"So the story of the cruelty of our horrible aunt probably won't work as a cover at the Haven," Joe concluded. "What else does the website say?"

I scanned it. "It says drugs and alcohol abuse by the teens," I told him.

"By the family, too, I bet," Joe commented.

"Yeah, that's on the list," I said. "Also step-family issues. Parents getting divorced. Fear of consequences for stuff like failing a test. Sometimes kids who have realized they're gay run, because they don't think their parents will be able to handle it."

"Stepfamily issues seems too complicated. We'd have to come up with step-sibs or stepparents," said Joe.

"Yeah. Too many fake details could trip us up. We should stay as close to the truth as we can," I agreed. I looked at the list of reasons to run again.

"If we go with drug or alcohol abuse—by us, I mean—we'd need to keep up the front that we're using."

"They've got to have rules against it at the Haven," Joe pointed out.

I nodded. "Except I bet there's some rule-breaking going on."

"How about divorce?"

"Works for me. So why are our parents getting divorced?" I asked. I felt a twinge zing down my back as the words came out of my mouth. It was creepy even thinking about our parents splitting up.

"Well, Mom does hate it when Dad forgets to turn his shirts right side out before he puts them in the laundry basket," said Joe.

"And Dad hates the way Mom has turned the entire basement into a recycling center," I added. "But . . ."

"It's not like anybody gets divorced over stuff like that. Or at least not unless there's a bunch of other badness going on," Joe finished for me.

"What if we use the alcohol abuse for Dad?" I asked. "We could say he lost his job, started drinking during the day. It got out of control."

"Okay," Joe said. "I guess we should throw some clothes and stuff in backpacks."

"Not too much, though," I cautioned. "I don't

think many runaways hit the streets with a pile of suitcases."

"No problem for me," Joe answered. "I'm not the clean underwear freak. You know my method—turn them inside out and they're pretty much fresh."

"And you wonder why girls like me more," I said. I stood up. "I'm going to get my stuff together. We'll leave in the morning."

"What excuse do we give Mom and Aunt Trudy this time?" asked Joe.

I thought about it for a minute. "Let's start with the truth. Let's tell them we're going to New York. We can say we're on the stage crew for the play our school is going to do at that teen one-act festival."

"Because a couple of the guys who were going to do it got the flu that's going around," Joe added.

"That should do it," I said.

Tomorrow night we'll be sleeping at the Haven, I thought. I wondered what we'd find out there. At least I knew I wouldn't be waking up without a kidney.

Well, I was pretty sure.

"Even with my eyes closed, I'd know we aren't in Bayport," Joe announced as we headed down West Twenty-third Street.

"You've got to be the reincarnation of Sherlock Holmes," I joked. "What gave it away? The smell of hot garbage mixed with old urine?" Every subway grate we passed was pumping out steam with that perfume.

"That, but you left out the scent of pretzels and hot dogs mixed with car exhaust," Joe answered. "With a little of the Hudson River added in. Oh, and aftershave, sweat . . ." He closed his eyes and sniffed. "A bit of wet dog, a bit of oil, new sneakers . . ."

"Definitely more variety of odors," I agreed.

"More variety of everything." Joe opened his eyes again. "More sounds, more kinds of food—I want to go to Little India, by the way. I need the aloo gobi in my belly. Then we can walk down to Little Italy and get cannoli for dessert, like that time when we were here with Mom and Dad."

"We're going to be undercover as runaways, not tourists. Or restaurant critics," I reminded him. "And speaking of being undercover . . ." I stopped next to a blanket laid out on the sidewalk. A guy had a bunch of stuff set out on it for sale. I picked up a blue and green plaid flannel shirt. The collar was frayed and one of the buttons was missing. Perfect.

"How much?" I asked the guy.

"A buck," he told me, without looking up from

the stack of records he was arranging. "All shirts are a buck."

I handed him a dollar and tossed the shirt to Joe.

"For me? You shouldn't have. You *really* shouldn't have," Joe said.

"It's for *work*," I told him.

Joe nodded. He took off his jacket and pulled the shirt on over his sweater. Then he grabbed a holey T-shirt with a faded picture of Britney Spears on the front and tossed it to me.

"No. Every guy in the place would want to beat me up if I walked around wearing this," I protested.

Joe studied the T-shirt for a minute. "Even I'd want to beat you up," he admitted. He put the shirt back and handed me a gray one with the words GARY'S CLAM SHACK on the front. It was too big and had permanent pit stains. I shrugged off my coat and added the short-sleeved T-shirt to the long-sleeved one I was already wearing.

"My gift to you," Joe said, paying the guy. The man grunted as he shoved the buck into his pocket, still working on getting his records in order. "Does anyone even buy records anymore?" Joe asked as we continued down the street.

"Collectors," I offered.

Joe glanced over his shoulder at the records on

the blanket. "I doubt many collectors shop off the sidewalk. At a flea market, maybe."

"At least he sold something today." I ran my hands over my new-to-me T-shirt. "With our two dollars he can get . . . a slice of pizza." And that was it.

"Good call on the clothes," Joe said.

"Yeah. I know we weren't exactly wearing our best, but I don't think we looked like we'd spent even a couple of days on the street."

"True. And I doubt many people take off from home and go directly to the Haven. It seems like running away is more of an impulse thing." Joe knelt down and pulled the lace out of one of his sneakers. "I think we need a little more distressing," he explained. "The shirts kind of stick out when everything else we have on is better."

I noticed a puddle of what I very much hoped was spilled soda. I ran my fingers though it, then wiped them on my jacket. "Aunt Trudy's going to kill me," I muttered.

"Hey, when you signed on with American Teens Against Crime, you knew there'd be danger," replied Joe.

We reached the corner. Joe and I were the only two who waited for the light to change. It's a New

York City thing. I'm surprised there isn't a fleet of ambulances that just circle the blocks waiting to pick up pedestrians who've been mowed down by taxis.

"There it is," Joe said, nodding toward a building in the middle of the block.

From this angle we could see a mural on the side of the Haven center that hadn't been visible in the footage we'd watched. A blond girl almost three stories tall was falling through a rabbit hole, her eyes wide and blank. Syringes and pills and wine bottles swirled around her. A leering Mad Hatter tore at her fluttering white apron. A rat gnawed at one of her little black shoes.

"I don't remember any rats in *Alice in Wonderland*," Joe commented.

"I think it's supposed to show what happens to runaways when they end up living on the street," I said.

"Deep."

"Let's get in there," I said.

Joe nodded and led the way up the three cement steps to the Haven's door. "Do we knock or—"

The door swung open before he could finish his question. A tall guy—he had to be six-three—with a scruff grinned down at us. "Welcome to the

Haven," he said. "You need a place to stay?" He ran his fingers over the little patch of hair under his lip.

"Yeah. We do," I answered. I expected him to ask for details, but he didn't. Which, when I thought about it, made sense. A lot of kids who run away probably have a lot of things they want to keep secret. If they got hit with a bunch of questions as soon as they walked into the place, they might bolt.

"We're pretty full up, but I think we can squeeze you in. Tess always says there's room for one more. Or, in this case, two. I'm Sandy, by the way." Joe and I took turns knocking fists with him. Then he waved us inside.

"Who's Tess?" asked Joe.

"Tess Markham. She runs the place. Founded it, actually. She had a son who took off when he was sixteen. It's been more than ten years, but I don't think she's ever completely given up hope that he'll come back," Sandy explained. He paused in the hallway and pointed to a large piece of poster board on the wall. It had a single word written on it in all capital letters: RESPECT. "We don't have a lot of rules here. This about does it." Sandy tapped the word.

"That covers a lot," he continued. "Respect

for the Haven. Respect for the other people who live here. Respect for yourselves. Respect for the Haven means you'll have assigned chores to keep the place clean and in good shape with repairs. Respect for the other people who live here means no stealing, no fighting, no trash talk. Also, no romantic relationships with other residents. When you're on your own and underage, that's plenty to deal with without the drama of having a boyfriend or girlfriend living in the house with you. Trust me on this one." Sandy gave us another one of his wide grins. "I stayed here when I first left home. Just dealing with school and job training was more than enough to keep me busy."

He tapped the word RESPECT again. "Like I said, respect includes respect for yourself. That means no drinking. No drugs. Tess tolerates a lot of things, but not being high while you're living at the Haven." He continued on down the hall. "This is my office," he told us.

Through the open door I saw a desk with mounds of paper and empty soda cans all over it. A lime green futon couch sat in front of it, along with a couple of mismatched chairs. "Feel free to drop by any time. You guys need to come by later so we can deal with some paperwork issues."

"What kind of paperwork?" I asked, trying to sound suspicious. If I was a real runaway, I wouldn't want to fill out any papers that would help anybody track me down.

"Don't worry. We keep all the info we get completely confidential," Sandy answered, as if he'd read my mind. "Mostly I want to talk to you guys about school and job training. We have GED classes and a bunch of different employment programs here. And Tess is awesome about getting kids college scholarships. I'll go through all the details with you later. First, lunch. Everyone who stays here takes a turn cooking, from the kids all the way up to Tess. She actually loves cooking. We practically have to shove her out of the kitchen on the nights she has some fundraising event set up. With the different cooks, some meals are better than others, but there's always lots of food."

He seems like a decent guy, I thought as we headed toward the dining hall. But there was something going on at the Haven that Evan had wanted to tell a reporter. Something bad. Sandy worked here. He'd even stayed here as a runaway. It would be almost impossible for him not to know about whatever it was Evan had found out. Right?

SUSPECT PROFILE

__Name:__ Sandy Lewis

__Hometown:__ Boston, Massachusetts

__Physical description:__ 6'3", approximately 210 lbs., age 27, light brown hair, brown eyes, scruff.

__Occupation:__ Assistant director, the Haven.

__Background:__ Lived at the Haven when he ran away from home as a teenager. Not in touch with his family.

__Suspicious behavior:__ His job gives him access to almost everything that goes on at the Haven. Whatever Evan wanted to report about the center was probably something Sandy knew. Would he kill to keep a secret about the Haven?

__Suspected of:__ The murder of Evan Davis.

__Possible motives:__ Sandy feels the Haven saved his life. He's loyal to the center and Tess Markham. He wouldn't want anything negative about the Haven to come out in the press.

"From the smell, I'd say that today's group of chefs have prepared spaghetti and garlic bread. Hard to mangle either of those too badly, so eat up in case the dinner crew decides to get a little creative," Sandy advised. He pushed open the double doors leading to the dining hall.

I froze. I saw something that could instantly end our mission.

4.

A DEAD GUY'S JACKET

Frank grabbed me by the arm and pulled me away from the door. What was the deal?

"Uh, is there a bathroom we could hit before lunch?" he asked Sandy.

"Down the hall, on the left," he answered.

"Come on," Frank told me.

"Are we girls now?" I asked as we walked down the hall. "Do we have to go to the bathroom in pairs?"

Frank glanced over his shoulder. I took a look too. The hall was empty. "I saw Lily Fowler in the dining room," Frank said.

"Lily Fowler? You mean elementary school Lily Fowler?" I asked.

"I'm pretty sure. She looks a lot different, but,

yeah, I'm almost positive it was her." Frank shoved his fingers through his dark hair. "If I recognized her . . ."

"Then she could recognize us," I finished for him.

"I'm not sure that she's going to buy that we're runaways, even with our cover story," said Frank. "If she remembers our family at all, it's probably not going to seem that likely."

"I was over at the Fowlers' a couple of times—for a birthday party and then to study with Lily and some other kids once. I met her parents and everything. I wouldn't have thought she'd end up at a place like the Haven," I answered.

Frank thought this over, then nodded. "True. I guess you never really know what it's like inside somebody else's family."

"So if she recognizes us, we just tell her the story we came up with—about Dad's drinking and everything. And if she doesn't, then we just act like we don't recognize her either," I said.

"Let's do it." Frank turned around and we walked back to the dining hall. I scanned the room as I stepped inside. Tables of different sizes were scattered around. A girl with a mole near the corner of her left eyebrow sat at the nearest one. "That's her," I said softly. When we'd known her, Lily had had reddish blond hair that fell halfway down her back. Now she practically had a crew cut, and her hair was ink black. But I knew that mole, and the tiny not-deep-enough-to-be-a-cleft indentation in her chin.

Okay, okay. I'd had a slight crush on her.

Lily must have felt me looking at her, because she glanced over. "Want to sit here?" she asked me and Frank. "There's room."

"Sure," I said. *She doesn't seem to recognize us*, I thought as Frank and I joined the group at Lily's table. "Thanks," I added.

"No prob." Lily grabbed an empty plate, loaded it up with spaghetti from the serving platter in the middle of the table, then passed it to me. She filled a plate for Frank next.

"Have you decided you're the table mom or what?" the guy next to Lily asked her.

Lily shrugged. "A few people were nice to me when I was the new meat. I thought I owed the universe a little payback. You have a problem with that, Jason?"

The guy, Jason, didn't answer. He just shoved a big forkful of spaghetti into his mouth and started chewing. The motion made the tattoo around his neck—a loop of barbed wire—slide up and down.

I wondered how I'd look with a tattoo. In Manhattan there had to be some true artists with the ink and needle. I could find one and—no, tats aren't good if you have to go undercover. There are times you have to look like a guy who'd never get a tattoo. And if you had to look like the kind of guy who wouldn't be caught dead without one, you could always go fake.

"So, have you been here long?" Frank asked Lily.

"About a month," she answered. "Jason has been here the longest—more than a year. Amy got here about a week before I did. " She gestured toward a girl whose curly blond hair was boinging out all over her head like it was made of springs.

"So what's it like? Is it an okay place?" asked Frank.

"It's safe. That's all that matters to me," Lily answered.

"Truth," Amy added. "Here I don't have to sleep with one eye open. That would be enough to make me give the place four stars. When you add in that it's warm, dry, clean, and doesn't smell disgusting, the rating goes up to five."

"You've been here the longest—what do you think?" I asked Jason.

He didn't answer. "Jason has a strict word quota," Lily told me. "He has to keep it under a hundred a day or his head explodes."

"Unbelievable," Jason muttered.

His one word didn't seem to be directed to Amy. Or me. I followed his gaze and saw a stocky guy heading into the dining hall.

"What?" asked Amy. "If you have enough words left to answer."

"That's Evan's jacket," Jason said. He jammed a piece of garlic bread into his mouth, his eyes never leaving Stocky Guy.

"That gives me the wiggin's." Amy gave an exaggerated shiver. "Walking around in a dead guy's jacket." She half stood. "That's nasty, Mark," she called out.

The stocky guy turned toward her in surprise. "What?" he asked.

"Evan's body's hardly cold and you're wearing his clothes?" Amy answered.

Mark grabbed the last empty chair at the table. Lily immediately got very busy putting a plate together for him.

"Evan gave me this jacket before he died," Mark explained. "It's not like I pulled it off his corpse or anything. And before you ask, yes, this is his five-dollar watch. He gave it to me too, along with about half the stuff in his backpack."

"Right. That makes sense," Jason challenged.

"It does make sense," Mark shot back. "Evan had just gotten that scholarship to art school in

California, remember? He wanted to start over. He didn't want anything that would remind him of New York. The guy probably would have gotten on the plane naked if he could have."

It seemed like Mark and Evan had been pretty tight. Had he known that Evan planned to talk to a reporter? Had he known what Evan wanted to talk to the reporter about? If Mark did know anything, he hadn't passed it along to the cops.

SUSPECT PROFILE

Name: Mark Hovde

Hometown: Washington, DC

Physical description: Brown hair worn in short ponytail, age 18, 5'9", approximately 210 lbs.

Occupation: In training program to become a bank teller.

Background: Ran away after his parents found out he was doing drugs. Sixty-two days clean.

Suspicious behavior: Knows a lot about Evan.

Suspected of: Having information about what led to Evan's death or of what Evan had found out about the Haven.

Possible motives: Afraid revealing the information could put him in danger.

"Why'd he jump, then?" Jason asked.

"He didn't jump!" Lily exclaimed, her voice high and shrill. "He would never kill himself! Never!"

Jason just grunted in reply.

"Evan died in an accident a few weeks ago," Amy explained to me and Frank. "He fell off a subway platform right before the train pulled in."

"Fell," Jason repeated. "Yeah, right."

Frank poured himself a glass of water. "Giving away stuff is classic suicidal behavior," he commented.

"Yeah, I knew this girl who killed herself once. At school the day before she did it, she was handing out her jewelry to people she'd hardly met," Amy volunteered. "Maybe Evan did off himself."

"Huh-uh. No," Lily insisted, her eyes bright and wet.

"You hardly knew him," protested Amy.

"You're right. I didn't. But I still know he wouldn't do anything like that," Lily replied.

Lily was way upset by even the suggestion that Evan had killed himself. It made me think she was close to him. Why was she pretending she wasn't? Did she know more than she was saying about how Evan really died?

Name: Lily Fowler

Hometown: Bayport, New Jersey

Physical description: Age 16, very short dyed black hair, blue eyes, mole at the end of left eyebrow, 5'3", approximately 115 lbs.

Occupation: Studying for her GED.

Background: Went to elementary school with Joe and Frank. Ran away from home five weeks ago after a fight with her mother. Lives at the Haven.

Suspicious behavior: Claims she barely knew Evan, but was very emotional when she talked about him.

Suspected of: Knowledge of the circumstances of Evan's death or of what Evan had found out about the Haven.

Possible motives: Afraid revealing what she knows would put her in danger. Protecting Evan's reputation.

"Every bed has a number," Mark told me and Frank. "You use the locker with the same number for your stuff." He pointed at the row of brightly painted lockers that stretched the length of one wall.

"Got it," Frank said.

"Sandy gave you that whole 'respect' speech already, right?" Mark asked.

"Soon as we walked in the door," I said.

"Yeah, well, that would be nice. But we don't live in Mister Rogers' Neighborhood, you know? If there's anything you want to make sure you hang on to, don't put it in the cubby. Keep it on you. That's what pretty much everybody does here."

"Anything else we should know?" I was hoping Mark would give us an idea of what Evan had found out about the Haven.

Mark shrugged. "Just watch your back. Trust no one, you know what I mean?" He headed out of the boys' dorm before Frank or I could ask another question.

"What do you think he—," I began. Then I noticed Frank had his "thinking" face on. It's the same look he has when he's constipated. Sorry. Too much information, right?

"In the video from the surveillance camera, I remember Evan holding a cardboard box when we first saw him, but the box wasn't in the evidence the police took from the tracks," Frank said.

I could picture the items that had been taken as evidence—a wallet, a piece of paper with the reporter's phone number, a little Swiss Army knife. "You're right."

Frank pulled on his coat. "Do you have the subway map from the piñata?"

"Yeah," I told him.

"I want to go to the station where Evan died," Frank announced.

5.
DOWN ON THE TRACKS

Joe and I trotted down the long flight of grimy cement steps leading into the subway. I couldn't help thinking that just a few weeks ago, Evan had been on these stairs—alive.

We walked over to the little booth outside the turnstiles. "Is there a lost and found here?" I asked the attendant.

"What'd you lose?" the attendant asked.

"A cardboard box about the size of a couple of shoe boxes," I told him. I hoped he wouldn't ask me what was inside.

He didn't. He pulled a plastic bin out from under the counter. "We got one glove. We got two knit hats. We got a coloring book." He rummaged around in the bin, digging deeper. "We got a cell

39

phone. We got some perfume, a couple of paper-back books. And that's it. No cardboard box."

"It was a long shot, anyway," I said to Joe.

"Let's look around a little more. Scene of the crime and everything," he suggested.

"*Possible* crime," I reminded him as he bought us each a MetroCard.

"Yeah, yeah, possible crime," he answered as swiped his card through the scanner and pushed through the nearest turnstile.

There weren't many people around. Early after-noon clearly wasn't a big travel time. We walked the length of the platform, peering down at the tracks as we went. There was plenty of litter down there: a high-heeled shoe, a half-eaten hot dog, newpapers, a few soda bottles.

"Nothing down there that's going to help us," Joe finally said.

"You're right. Let's go back to the Haven. We need to gather more evidence there," I said as we headed back toward the turnstiles.

"That means talking to Lily some more," Joe answered. "I got the feeling she was closer to Evan than she says she was. Did you notice how upset she got about the idea that he committed suicide?"

I nodded. "We definitely need to find out more about Lily. Mark, too."

"Yeah, he seemed like he was pretty good friends with Evan," said Joe.

"And he told us to watch our backs. It made me think he could know some of the bad stuff about the Haven," I noted.

"Like whatever Evan was going to tell that reporter. Good—" Joe stopped midsentence and grabbed my arm. "Check out the homeless guy at three o'clock. Does that box look familiar to you?"

I glanced to the left. A man—I couldn't tell if he was nearer my age or my dad's—lay on a sheet of cardboard. He used a pink down jacket, clearly a woman's, as a blanket. Near his chest was a cardboard box—about the size of the one we'd seen Evan carrying—and a collection of other stuff.

"Could be it," I told Joe. We veered toward the man. He sat up as we approached.

"Hi," I said. "I think that box might be the one a friend of mine lost about two weeks ago. Would it be okay if I look in it and check?"

"No, it wouldn't be okay," the man answered. "It's mine."

"We don't want to take it away from you," Joe assured him. "We just want to look inside."

"If I was one of those so-called regular people, you wouldn't be asking that," the man said. "If

I was waiting for a train in a suit, you wouldn't come over and ask if you could paw through my briefcase. I'd have security haul you off if you tried it."

Standoff. Now what?

"How about if we pay you?" Joe asked. He pulled out his wallet. "I have twenty bucks. It's yours if you let us look in the box for, like, fifteen minutes."

The man snorted. "You think that would work on the suit with the briefcase? I'll tell you what. It wouldn't. And it's not going to work on me, either. This is my personal property."

"I'm not sure it is," Joe burst out. "I'm not saying you stole it. But I think you might have found it down here in the station." He reached for the box.

The man leaped to his feet with the box in his arms. "You're not getting it." He ran toward the tracks. Joe and I looked at each other, then chased after him. When he got to the lip of the platform, the man didn't hesitate. He leaped right off. Joe and I looked at each other again, a longer look this time. Then we jumped down onto the tracks.

That box could lead us to the truth about Evan's death. We couldn't let it out of our sight. We ran after the man, into the subway tunnel. After a few seconds, my eyes adjusted to the darkness, but I still didn't see the man anywhere. "Where'd he go?" I called to Joe as I skidded to a stop.

"I don't see him," Joe answered.

Cautiously we walked deeper into the tunnel, scanning the shadows. I caught a flash of movement against one of the metal pillars. I squinted. Yeah, it was him. "Look, we didn't tell you the whole truth," I called out. My voice didn't sound at all familiar as it echoed through the empty space.

I moved toward him. Slowly. I didn't want him to bolt again. "We're not just trying to get back something a friend lost. The guy the box belonged to—if it's even his—is dead."

"We think he might have been murdered," added Joe.

The man emerged from behind the pillar and took a few steps toward us. "Murdered?"

"Yeah," I said. "My brother and I are trying to figure out who did it."

"We think the guy—his name was Evan—had that box with him the day he died. We think it might have something in it that will help us find out whether somebody killed him or his death was an accident," Joe explained.

"If you were a guy in a suit, we'd be saying the same thing. We'd be asking you to help us. Will you help us? All we want is to find out how our friend died," I said.

"You should have told me that in the first place," the man answered. "I'm a believer in truth, justice, and the American way—just like Superman." He handed me the box. "I just don't like to be pushed around."

He turned and headed deeper into the subway.

"Where's he going?" Joe whispered. "The Batcave?"

"Wrong superhero," I answered. "Wherever he's going, I don't . . ."

The words evaporated in my mouth—my suddenly dry mouth. The air around me was . . . vibrating. Then the ground started to shake.

Two small circles of blinding light appeared in the darkness.

"Train!" yelled Joe.

6.
LET JOE DO IT

The train horn let out a long blast. The sound broke my paralysis. I stumbled back and pressed my body against the tunnel wall. Frank was right beside me.

The flesh of my cheeks flapped as the train rushed by, discharging hot, noxious air. I didn't care how bad it smelled—I sucked in a deep lungful. Then I looked over at Frank. "That was fun. Let's wait for one more train to go by. I want to do it again!"

Frank gave me this disgusted big-brother look, then started walking toward the mouth of the tunnel. He never knows when I'm kidding. It's 'cause he has no sense of humor himself. Want proof? He doesn't think the Three Stooges are funny. That says it all.

As soon as I stepped back into the light of the subway station, I grabbed the edge of the platform—the sweet, sweet platform—with both hands and hoisted myself up. Frank handed me the box, then pulled himself up next to me.

The weird thing was, nobody said anything. The station wasn't crowded, but there were people around. And they all acted like it was totally normal for two guys to come climbing out from the subway tracks. It's not even like we were wearing uniforms or anything.

That's something I've noticed on other visits to New York. It's like the people here pride themselves on the fact that nothing can surprise them. It's the ultimate been-there-done-that attitude.

Frank and I walked over to the closest bench and sat down with the box between us. "I hope this thing actually is the one we saw Evan carrying," my brother said.

"I hope he didn't just use the box to hold his dirty laundry," I added. Frank didn't laugh, because of the no-sense-of-humor thing. He just pulled open the cardboard flaps.

I peered inside. The only thing in there was a bunch of photographs printed on sheets of oversize paper. "Guess he couldn't find an envelope," I muttered.

Frank gathered the pictures into a stack and took them out. I leaned closer so I could see the one on top: a shot of Evan sitting on the stoop in front of a tiny grocery store. He was holding out a paper cup as an impatient-looking woman stuck a buck into it. The next photo showed Evan sleeping on a park bench. The next showed him rooting through a garbage can in the park.

"Was someone following him?" asked Frank. "It doesn't look like he knew he was being photographed."

"He definitely wasn't saying 'cheese' in any of these," I agreed.

Frank flipped to the next picture. It showed Evan picking a man's pocket. The next showed him boosting an iPod from an electronics store. "That's it. The last one," Frank said. "What do these tell us?"

"It seems like they were taken over at least several days," I commented. "The weather is different. And Evan's wearing two different shirts."

"The photographer—assuming all the pictures were taken by the same person—must have known a lot about Evan. They'd have to have been around him for at least a few days, like you said. Who knows what they saw that isn't in the pictures."

"They might have seen Evan with his killer," I agreed.

"If the photographer isn't the killer himself," Frank pointed out. "Whoever took these pictures was extremely interested in him."

"You think his parents hired a PI to find him?" I asked.

"Possibly. They do look sort of like surveillance photos." Frank started flipping through the pictures again.

"Hold up," I exclaimed. "Go back one—to the picture of Evan sleeping on the park bench."

Frank went back to that picture. "Look in Evan's sunglasses," I told him.

"Good call," said Frank. "You can see a reflection of the person who took the picture in the right lens." He traced the reflection with one finger. "It's hard to see much detail."

"But we know it's a her, not a him," I answered. "A her with red hair."

"It's a start," Frank said. "More than we had before, anyway. Let's see if we can find out where this picture was taken."

We headed over to an old guy waiting for the train. "Excuse me, does this park look familiar to you?" Frank asked.

"No," the old guy answered, even though he'd barely glanced at the photo.

"Let me see it," said a woman with a leopard-print scarf and gloves.

"Thanks," Frank told her as we walked over. He held out the picture.

"Washington Square Park," she said. "You can see part of the arch. Any real New Yorker should have been able to tell you that." She shot an irritated look at the old man, then turned back to me and Frank. "So you must be new in town."

"You're a real detective," I joked.

Frank rolled his eyes. "We're on vacation. Can you tell us how to get to Washington Square Park from here?"

She rattled off directions and pretty much a billion details about the park that we didn't need to know, then added, "And don't eat from the little food carts on the street. You know what the locals call them? Roachmobiles."

"Gross," I said.

"Thanks again," Frank told her. Then we were outta there. Back through the turnstiles, up the stairs, and out into the somewhat fresh air. We started to walk downtown, passing this big metal cube thing that I think was supposed to be art.

When we turned the corner, I spotted the huge

cement arch. The woman who was an expert on all things New York had told us it was built to celebrate the centennial of George Washington's inauguration.

Washington Square Park isn't much of a park, if you ask me. There aren't many trees. There's not even all that much grass. There are a lot of pigeons, though. I guess birds are parklike.

"Can I just say 'bingo'?" Frank asked.

"I would really prefer that you didn't," I told him.

Did I mention Frank is corny? Seriously, when was the last time you heard anyone say "bingo"— when they aren't actually playing bingo? Actually, when was the last time you saw anyone play bingo?

"Okay, well, can I just say that I think the girl in the picture is right over there?" I followed his gaze and saw a red-haired girl who definitely seemed like she could match the reflection we saw in Evan's glasses in that one photo. She was sitting by a fountain playing a guitar. A couple of other teenagers hung around, listening.

"Feel like listening to some music?" I asked Frank.

"Definitely," he answered.

We wandered over to the girl. She smiled at us

and kept on playing. All right, she smiled at Frank. He blushed. I was ignored. Same old, same old.

Everyone around gave her a little applause when she finished up the song. "Thank you, thank you," she said. Then she smiled at me. You heard right, *me*. Which is how it should be. I *am* the cuter brother. I'm blond and everything.

"I see my fame is spreading," the girl said, winking at me—or possibly Frank. "I've got some new fans today."

"You were great," I told her. "What's your name? You know, so I can buy your CD." I guess I can be a little corny myself at times.

The girl laughed. "Olivia Gorman. And my new CD will be out . . . in my dreams."

"No way, Liv. It's gonna happen for you—soon," a guy with a faux hawk told her.

"Yeah. You're going to be the next teen sensation," added a girl with a grin. She popped a bubble-gum bubble.

"It's going to have to happen *extremely* soon, then," Olivia answered. "I'm turning the big two-oh in a couple of months."

"Oh. I didn't know you were that old," Bubble-Gum Girl teased. "Do your thing on the new boys!" she added.

"What thing?" asked Frank.

"Olivia's practically psychic. She guesses people's names. Where they're from. What they're into. It's amazing," Bubble-Gum Girl explained.

"I'm about as psychic as a rock." Olivia put her guitar back in its case. "What I am is observant." She narrowed her eyes at Frank. "Hmm. You definitely come from the suburbs—and not the burbs like Queens. Out-of-state burbs. Your brother, too, of course."

"How'd you know we're brothers?" I burst out.

"You have the same hair line," Olivia answered. "See, I'm observant. Now, names . . ."

She was interrupted by another girl bounding up to her. The girl reminded me of a chocolate lab: glossy brown hair and big brown eyes. "Look what I got!" she exclaimed. She lifted her shirt, flashing her belly—and the wallet shoved in the waistband of her jeans.

"Shay, we have company. Say hi to, um, Robert and Joe," Olivia told the girl, shooting her a "nice going, idiot" look.

"Oh. Hi. I didn't notice you guys," Shay told us. "Which of you is Robert and which is Joe?"

"I'm Joe," I said.

"And I'm Frank," he said, answering Shay, but looking at Olivia.

Olivia shrugged. "I'm not always right. If I was,

I'd be mega-rich. I'd have a loft in SoHo instead of sleeping in the park."

"Speaking of money." Shay reached under her shirt, fumbled around for a minute, then handed Olivia thirty dollars.

"Shay, what part of 'we have company' didn't you understand?" Olivia asked, exasperated.

"They don't care that I picked a wallet," she answered. "Do you, you guys?"

I shrugged. "None of my business."

"Mine either," Frank added.

"My nonpsychic psychicness tells me that neither of you have entered a life of crime yourself, though. Am I right?" Olivia raised one eyebrow. She did it really well.

"Uh, not exactly," I said.

"Well, you've only been living alfresco for less than a week. Am I right?" Olivia asked.

"Huh?" I replied. The nonpsychic psychic girl had kind of lost me.

"Alfresco—outdoors," Frank told me. "You are good," he said to Olivia. "We are currently without roof. But only the last few days."

"Well, when you get hungry enough, you might need to know how to boost a wallet. Here's the rundown. You carry your jacket or a newspaper to hide your hand movements. A baby's even better, but we don't have one available." She smiled. "Then you do something like drop some change or a bag near the mark. When he bends down to help you pick it up, you pick his pocket. You can also just bump into the mark. Make sure to apologize, though. Don't just take off," Olivia explained. "Who wants to try it first? You?" she asked me.

"Do it, Joe," Bubble-Gum Girl urged.

I hesitated. I wasn't going to find out how Evan died if I was sitting in jail. But . . . Evan had a connection to Olivia. It would be easier to find out what kind of connection if she trusted me and Frank.

"I'll help you choose the mark," said Olivia. "That's the tricky part." She scanned the people in the park.

"The guy in the tie!" Bubble-Gum cried. "We could all have lunch for a week on what he paid for it. He's got to have fat wads of cash."

Olivia shook her head. "It's a knockoff. And the shoes—they're trying very hard to look like Ralph Lauren. But they cost about thirty bucks. Plus the heels are worn down, and he hasn't coughed up the three dollars it would cost to fix them. I'd say he has at most a twenty-dollar bill."

"That guy isn't faking," Faux Hawk commented, jerking his chin toward a twentysomething blond guy.

"Sunglasses alone cost four hundred smackers," Olivia agreed. "Marc Jacobs. This year's collection."

"So go," Faux Hawk told me.

"No," Olivia said sharply. "He spends serious time at the gym. He does it just so he'll have pretty abs and all that. But he thinks it makes him tough. He'll put up a fight. He won't put up a good fight—because all he's used to punching is a bag. But he'll make a crazy loud scene."

Olivia took another look at the park crowd. "Him." She nodded toward an older guy in a fedora.

"Him?" Faux Hawk shook his head. "Talk about worn-down shoes."

"He's careful with his money. And he's not vain," Olivia explained. "And he's old-fashioned. No credit cards for him. When he buys something, he pulls out a nice stack of cash. Never leaves home without it. I'm thinking four-fifty or five hundred."

I watched the man head across the park. Was Olivia right about him? Or any of the other people she'd analyzed?

"He's getting away," Shay said. "I'll do him."

"No, let Joe do it," answered Olivia.

"I'm there," I told her.

7.
BUMP AND PICK

I watched Joe—trying not to look like I was watching—as he fell in behind the man with the fedora. I couldn't believe my brother was going to try to pick his pocket. I got why he was doing it. He was trying to make Olivia trust us. But I wasn't sure it was a good idea.

"And Joe is making his move," the guy with the faux hawk said, his voice hushed, like the announcer for a golf tournament. "He's going for the bump-and-pick method. Nice bump. Very natural."

A *click* jerked my attention away from Faux Hawk and over to Olivia. She'd just snapped a picture of Joe. "His first wallet has to be commemorated," she told me.

I looked over at Joe. He was standing close to the

56

man, apologizing to him for bumping into him.

"This is the key moment. If the mark is going to notice that his pocket feels light, he's probably going to notice it now," Faux Hawk continued.

I wanted to run over there and . . . do *something*. I'm the older brother. It felt so wrong standing there watching Joe stealing.

"But no, the mark is walking away. Oblivious. And Joe is coming back a winner. Wait. No. The mark has stopped walking. Has he realized what just happened?" asked Faux Hawk, still doing his golf announcer voice, like it was no big deal.

I took a quick glance at the man. I didn't want to make him suspicious by staring.

He was tying his shoe. That was it.

"False alarm," Faux Hawk said. "It was only the matter of a simple untied shoelace. The mark is now exiting the park. Won't he be surprised when he tries to pay for his taxi on the way home tonight?"

"Let's see it," said Olivia when Joe returned to the group.

Joe flashed his stomach just the way Shay had. Olivia reached out and snagged the wallet. She opened it, did a quick count. "Four hundred and sixty bucks. Am I good or what?" She took out a twenty, then grinned at Joe. "My fee, since I picked out a good fishie for you."

"Sounds fair to me," Joe said, and Olivia tossed the wallet back to him. Then she pointed at me. "You're up, Frank who looks like a Robert."

There was no way. "Not on an empty stomach," I said quickly. "Joe, you're going to buy me a hot dog with some of your cash, right?"

"I'll even buy you two, my brother," answered Joe. "Let's go find a roachmobile."

We started across the patchy grass before Olivia could protest. "Hey, guys," she called. I glanced over my shoulder but didn't stop walking. "If you get tired of being roofless, there's a decent shelter, just for teenagers. The Haven, over on West Twenty-third."

That got a full stop out of me. "If it's so great, why are you sleeping in the park?" I asked.

Olivia shrugged. "I'm a free spirit. That place has too many rules. But two boys fresh out of the burbs probably wouldn't mind."

"Maybe we'll check it out," Joe put in. "We need to find a police station," he said when we were out of Olivia and company's earshot.

I nodded. "To turn in the wallet."

"I guess I'll have to eat the twenty Olivia took," Joe complained. He transferred a twenty from his wallet into the stolen one.

"I was afraid you were going to get caught for a second," I admitted.

"*You* were afraid? I was expecting an alarm to go off the second I touched the guy," Joe said. "But I got the skills. If I wasn't such a good guy I could have a nice, cushy life of crime going."

"Really. So, evil genius, did you even realize that Olivia took your picture while you were robbing that man?" I asked.

"No way!" Joe exclaimed.

"Yeah. I wonder if that's the way it happened with Evan," I said.

"Seems pretty likely."

"But what did she want with them?" I shook my head. "Usually you'd use pictures like that to blackmail someone. But blackmailing a guy living in a center for runaway teens doesn't make any sense. Evan can't have had much money."

"Maybe she used the pictures to force him to keep on stealing and giving her a cut. Maybe she told him she'd turn him in if he didn't," Joe offered.

"That makes sense to me," I said. "What if she was blackmailing Evan and he tried to turn it around on her? What if he threatened to expose the way she ropes other homeless kids into stealing for her?"

"And what if she decided to kill him before he did?" asked Joe.

Name: Olivia Gorman

Hometown: Bakersfield, California

Physical description: Age 19, long red hair, 5'9", approximately 140 lbs., tattoo of the queen of hearts on left shoulder blade.

Occupation: Thief

Background: Wants to be a musician.

Suspicious behavior: Took pictures of Evan committing crimes.

Suspected of: Blackmailing Evan. Possibly killing him.

Possible motives: Blackmailing him for money. Murdering him to keep him from exposing her.

Joe and I headed into the Haven's common room. We figured that would be a good place to get a sense of how the other kids felt about the center.

I did a quick survey. Lily, Amy, and a couple of other girls were watching *Dr. Phil*. Another girl was sitting on a beanbag, reading. Five kids seemed to be studying for the GED at one table. Mark and a few other people were playing poker at another table.

"You guys want in?" Mark called, noticing us standing near the doorway.

"You ready to lose a lot of paper clips?" Joe asked. That's what they were using for poker chips—paper clips.

"Bring it on," answered Mark as Joe and I took the two empty seats at the table. He gave us thirty paper clips each to start us off, and then he did basic intros. "Frank. Joe. Sean. Rosemary," he said, pointing as he called out the names. "Ante up."

Sean, Rosemary, and Mark tossed two paper clips into the center of the table. Joe and I did too.

Rosemary dealt. I tried to keep an ear on the other conversations going on around me as I looked at my cards. I had one pair. And the pair? Twos. But I wasn't here to win. I was here to get information.

We started the first round of bidding. "I'm putting up five of the shiny ones," Sean said when it was his turn.

"Somebody's feeling confident," commented Rosemary.

"You want to know my secret?" Sean asked.

"I guess," Rosemary told him. "Although, as you know, you're always banished to the losers' lounge before I am."

"I don't care if I win or lose. I'm outta here. And pretty soon I'll be playing with cash instead of paper clips," Sean bragged.

"What? You found one of Willy Wonka's golden tickets and he's going to give you the candy factory?" Mark asked sarcastically.

"Pretty much," answered Sean. "Tess just told me she's taking me to a fund-raiser tomorrow to get money for me to go to school. She's taking over this place called Earl Grey's for a private party. They do a whole extreme tea thing. Little sandwiches and like that. Plus a million kinds of tea. Tess has invited a bunch of high-society types. By the time they're on their second cup, I'll have enough cash to go to college and vet school."

Mark stood up and shoved all his paper clips into Sean's pile. "That's my contribution. It's more than you're gonna get from your tea party." He stalked off.

"What's his problem?" Sean muttered. "He been dipping into the pills again or what?"

Rosemary shook her head. "He's been doing really good staying clean. Maybe he started thinking about Evan. It sucks so bad that Evan died before he could use the money Tess got him to go to art school. He was so talented. He did that mural on the side of the building."

I discarded everything but my pair and ended up adding a second pair to my hand. Nice. Joe raised—again. No surprise. He does that no matter what he's holding.

"So does this happen a lot? Tess raising money for kids to go to school?" I asked as Sean dealt.

"She's always trying to raise money for the kids here. I don't think she even sleeps," said Rosemary. "You heard about her son, right?"

"Yeah," Joe answered.

"I think that's why she works so hard. It's like when she finds a bed for a kid or gets money for one of us to go to school, she's doing it for him. It's like we're all replacements for her son—especially Sandy," Rosemary told us.

"Our own Dr. Phil," commented Sean.

"Did you see how she was dressed when she went to that black-tie dinner she set up for Evan?" one of the girls watching TV asked. "Her polyester dress and cheapo plastic purse."

"So what, Karen?" Rosemary said. "So what if Tess doesn't care about clothes? She has more important things to think about."

"She could think about them while wearing something not embarrassing," Karen shot back.

"How does she decide which kid she's going to do one of these fund-raising things for?" I asked.

Tess sounded like a great lady, but she ran the Haven. How could she be in charge and not at least know about whatever trouble Evan had discovered?

"Tess always says that it's her goal to get every kid a scholarship. Every kid who wants one, anyway," Lily explained. "She also has job training programs for people who don't want to go to college."

"Do you want to go?" I asked. I was still having

SUSPECT PROFILE

Name: Tess Markham

Hometown: Charlotte, North Carolina

Physical description: Age 54, short silver hair, black eyes, 5'9", approximately 160 lbs.

Occupation: Director of the Haven.

Background: Son ran away ten years ago.

Suspicious behavior: Runs the Haven, so probably knows or is involved in whatever Evan found out.

Suspected of: Being involved in something illegal. Killing Evan.

Possible motives: To protect the Haven from the bad publicity Evan was about to give the center.

trouble wrapping my mind around the fact that Lily Fowler was living at the Haven. What had happened in her life to get her here?

Lily shrugged. "Right now, I'm in day-to-day mode. What about you? Are you planning to be a cop like your—" She snapped her mouth closed for a moment, then went on. "It seems like half the guys I meet want to be cops like, uh, your basic action heroes."

But that's not what she had been about to say. She'd stopped herself from asking if I wanted to be a cop like my dad.

Lily had recognized me and Joe. Why was she pretending she hadn't? What was she hiding?

8.
SECRETS

"So what do you think Lily's deal is?" I asked. Frank and I had ducked into the empty dining hall so we could talk without being overheard.

"Maybe she's embarrassed," said Frank. "Maybe she doesn't want us to know that she ended up here."

"But we ended up here," I pointed out.

Frank shoved his hands through his hair. "True," he admitted. "So . . . maybe she thinks we'd tell her parents where she is if we remembered her. Maybe she was hoping that if she acted like she didn't know us, we wouldn't recognize her. It's been a while since elementary school."

"Again, we're in the same situation she is. We're

supposedly runaways too. Why would we turn in somebody else who'd run?" I asked.

"You're right," said Frank. "All I know is Lily's behavior is suspicious. She's definitely keeping secrets, and we need to know if they have anything to do with Evan."

"So what's the deal with Lily?" I asked everyone at my table that night at dinner.

"My brother has a crush," Frank added.

"I just think she's cool," I protested.

"She's very cool. I don't think I want to help you get close to her," joked Sean.

"I'll give you the Lily scoopage," said Nina, one of the girls who'd been watching TV with Lily. "She's from Minnesota. Raised by a single mom. Mom hooked up with a guy who was not kid-friendly. Mom kicked Lily out. Very nice, huh?"

Very false, I thought. I didn't know about the rest of it, but Lily definitely wasn't from Minnesota. And last I knew, she had two parents, including a mom who wasn't the mean type.

"How'd she end up here?" I asked.

"New York here or the Haven here?" Nina asked back.

"Either. Both," I said.

"Her mom gave her a little dough to start out on. Lily figured Manhattan would be the coolest place to live. And she's right," Nina answered. "She figured she'd be able to find a job and get a place before she ran out of money. But the only jobs were McJobs, and you can't even buy a piece of cardboard to sleep on with what they pay. So she ended up sleeping on the subway, just riding all night. Then she met Olivia, and Olivia sent her here."

"We met Olivia. She told us about this place too," Frank said.

"She sends everybody here. She's kind of like the big sister to every homeless kid she meets," explained Nina.

"What does Lily—," I began.

"Don't get your hopes up, Sparky," another girl, Erin, interrupted. "Lily's boyfriend just died. There's no way she's going to ready for a new guy for a looong time."

"What are you talking about?" Nina asked. "Lily never told me anything about a boyfriend."

"And Nina's a top interrogator," said Sean. "One conversation and she can suck out the contents of your brain."

"Well, you must have missed a little of Lily's gray matter," Erin told Nina. "She and Evan had a thing going. I can't believe you didn't know that."

"There's no way. I never saw them together. Not even once," Sean protested. "And I hung with Evan a lot."

"I walked in on them making out in the supply closet once," Erin said. "They asked me not to say anything, so I didn't. I know how to keep my mouth shut—unlike some people," she added, looking at Nina.

"Why would they care if people knew they were together?" I asked.

"Did you forget your orientation already? No romantic attachments," said Nina. "That's probably why they didn't ever eat together or sit together in the common room or anything." Nina speared a cucumber out of her salad and stuck it on the side of her plate. "They were probably afraid Tess or Sandy would have made them break up."

After dinner, Frank and I sat in the common room watching *Project Runway*. The girls had gotten control of the remote again. Didn't matter. What I really wanted to watch was Lily, and she was sitting on the floor a few feet away from me.

Frank and I were waiting for a chance to talk to her—alone. But it didn't seem like she was planning on moving away from her friends for a while. They were yelling at the TV screen and arguing about who deserved to get kicked off.

I was getting itchy. And Frank looked like was about to slip into a fashion-induced coma. So I decided to make a move. I leaned close to Lily. "Mr. Orr would be pretty disappointed to see where we ended up, huh?" I said into her ear.

Lily jerked her head toward me so fast that her cheekbone cracked against my nose. "Sorry," she said automatically.

"It's okay," I answered.

"I need to—I've got to—" Lily jumped up and hurried out of the room. I elbowed Frank and we rushed after her. We caught up to her in the empty hallway.

"Lily, can we talk to you for a second?" asked Frank.

Reluctantly she turned to face us. "I didn't think you guys recognized me."

"You haven't changed that much," I said.

Lily gave a harsh bark of laughter. "Since the sixth grade? Thanks a lot."

"No, I mean, of course you've changed. Your hair's a different color, and you're—" I hesitated, then started up again. "But you're still you, enough you for me to know it was you," I said, stumbling over my explanation. And I'm always saying how *Frank* gets flustered around girls.

"I knew it was you, too," Lily admitted. "Both of you. I knew it the second you walked into the dining hall."

"So why'd you pretend you didn't?" Frank asked.

"It just seemed less . . . complicated," she said. "I just don't feel like that Bayport Lily anymore. Or the Concord, Massachusetts, Lily. That's where we moved after sixth grade."

"I get that," I said.

Lily gave that harsh laugh again. "Sure you do," she said. "Come on. You guys don't really belong here. You're working on a case, right?"

Lily didn't know Frank and I were with ATAC. Nobody outside the agency did. But Frank and I had a reputation in Bayport for being amateur detectives. We'd solved a bunch of mysteries in our hometown.

I glanced at Frank. He gave me a little nod. It seemed like it was best to tell the truth—at least part of the truth.

"Yeah. We're working on a case. That's why we wanted to talk to you," I said.

"And we wanted to see how you are, too. Are you okay?" I added quickly.

"Pretty much," Lily answered. "This is a pretty safe place. And that's all I'm really looking for right now. I guess sometime I'll have to figure out a plan. But right now, all I want is a place where no one will bother me. There aren't many of those around when you're a teenage girl with no money in this city—or anywhere else, I guess."

She frowned, and I noticed a sheen of moisture coating her eyes. Was she about to cry?

"It used to be better here. I was almost sort of, you know, happy," Lily added.

"Before Evan died?" I asked.

Lily blinked rapidly, clearing away the unshed tears. "What do you know about Evan?" she demanded.

"We know how he died. We know it might not have been an accident," Frank said. "That's why we're here."

"You think his dad killed him, don't you?" Lily burst out. "That's what I think. I just have no way to prove it. You guys have to find a way to put him in jail for the rest of his life."

"Evan's dad? Why would Evan's father want him dead?" I asked.

"Do you even know who Evan's father is?" said Lily.

"We hardly know anything about Evan's background. Anything you can tell us would be a huge help," Frank told her.

"Evan's dad is running for mayor in Long Island. And Evan . . . he did some not exactly legal stuff when he was living on the streets. There are times when you pretty much have to, just to survive," Lily explained.

"You think Evan's father killed him just to protect his political career?" I asked.

"Just? His career is all Evan's dad cares about," Lily answered.

"Did you ever meet him?" Frank said.

"Only once," Lily said. "But I heard all about him from Evan. As soon as I heard how Evan died, I was sure it wasn't an accident. I was sure his father had something to do with it. Maybe he didn't actually push Evan in front of the train himself. But he wanted it done. He made it happen. I know it."

"Evan had an appointment with a reporter the day he died. That's why he was in the subway station in the first place—to get to the meeting. Do you have any idea what he wanted to talk to her about?" asked Frank.

Lily's brow furrowed. "He didn't tell me anything about that. And he told me everything."

"We think he was planning to talk to the reporter about something he'd found out about the Haven," I said. "Something bad. Did Evan ever talk to you about anything like that?"

The lines in Lily's forehead deepened. "No. I mean, we used to complain about Tess, how she has that rule about no hookups between the kids living here. Evan and I had to be really careful about not being seen together too much. It was a pain."

"That's it? Nothing else?" Frank prodded.

"Yeah," Lily answered. "There were other little things about the place that neither of us liked. You have to keep a close eye on your stuff. Sometimes the food sucks. Nothing big. Nothing reporter-worthy." She did the rapid blinking thing again. "I can't believe Evan would keep anything big a secret from me. I don't understand. . . ."

"He was probably going to tell you about it when he got back," I said. I had no idea if it was true or not. But I wanted to make her feel better.

"Maybe." Lily used the back of her little finger to wipe under her eyes. "I'm glad you guys are here," she said. "I want Evan's dad to pay for what he did."

"We'll go talk to him. Do you have his address?" Frank asked.

"Yeah, I went there with Evan once," said Lily. "Evan wanted to make things right with his dad. He wanted to see if he could move back home. But his father told him to forget about that. He

SUSPECT PROFILE

<u>Name:</u> Martin Davis

<u>Hometown:</u> Lake Ronkonkoma, New York

<u>Physical description:</u> Thinning blond hair, 5'11", approximately 170 lbs., scar across left thumb pad.

<u>Occupation:</u> Aspiring politician

<u>Background:</u> High school valedictorian. Top of his class at Harvard Law. Youngest partner at the law firm.

<u>Suspicious behavior:</u> Told Evan he never wanted to see him again, that the best thing Evan could do was leave him alone.

<u>Suspected of:</u> Killing Evan or having him killed.

<u>Possible motives:</u> Thought Evan could ruin his political career.

said he never wanted to see Evan again. It was horrible. You should have seen Evan's face."

"We promise we'll find out the truth," I told Lily.

9.
GET OUT!

"Evan's dad is pretty popular around here," I commented. I nodded toward an ELECT MARTIN DAVIS sign in the front yard of the house we were passing. We'd seen about thirteen of them since we got off the Long Island Rail Road at the Lake Ronkonkoma station. Plus there were posters stapled to telephone poles and taped in store windows.

"How bad do you think Mr. Martin's chances would be hurt if it came out that Evan was a runaway and had done some stealing while he was living on the streets?" Joe shifted Evan's cardboard box under his arm. "Enough to cost him the election?"

"Maybe. That article I was reading on the train said the race is pretty close. Although we seem to be in Davis town right now," I answered.

"Well, we are getting pretty close to his house," Joe reminded me. "It should be on the next block."

"Right. Anyway, who knows how many votes he'd lose," I said. "I'm sure some of his supporters would still back him. But some people might think that if a man can't manage his own family, he definitely won't be able to manage a town as mayor."

"This is a heartless question, but do you think Evan's death will have any effect on how the votes come out?" Joe pointed out another ELECT MARTIN DAVIS sign.

I thought about it for a minute. "Not in a negative way," I said slowly. "Actually, and this is a heartless answer, it might even get him some sympathy votes."

"Still, it's hard to imagine anybody would kill their own kid," Joe observed.

"It's happened before. But, yeah, it is hard to believe." I stopped and looked across the street at a big Victorian house with a perfectly manicured lawn and a new paint job. "That's Mr. Davis's place."

"Let's get to it," said Joe.

We crossed the street and headed up the walkway to the front door. I rang the bell.

Mr. Davis opened it himself, which sort of surprised me. I thought he'd be out shaking hands and kissing babies. "Hello. I'm Frank Hardy, and this is my brother, Joe," I told him. "We're friends of Evan's." Joe and I had decided that was the simplest explanation for our showing up at Mr. Davis's door.

"We're really sorry about what happened to Evan," Joe added.

"I appreciate that," said Mr. Davis. "Would you like to come in for a minute?"

"Thanks," I said as Mr. Davis ushered us inside.

"Take a seat," Mr. Davis told us, waving toward the living room. "I'll get us something to drink. Soda okay?"

"Sure," answered Joe. He and I headed over to the big snow-white sofa.

"I don't think our pants are clean enough for that." I sat in a wooden rocking chair.

"It's got to be killing you not to be able to wear clean clothes every day," Joe joked. He plopped down in an armchair. A brown one. "Have you been trying my underwear method?"

I ignored him. Sometimes that's all you can do with Joe. Instead of answering, I scanned the room. There weren't any signs of life. No books out. No

78

shoes lying around. No empty glasses or anything. *Aunt Trudy would love this place*, I thought.

"Check out the mantel," Joe said.

"What about it?" I asked.

"No pictures. No family pictures anywhere around," he answered.

"Well, Lily said Evan's mom died a long time ago," I reminded him.

"Still, it's—" Joe broke off as Mr. Davis came in.

"The couch scared you, huh?" he asked as he handed us glasses of soda.

"It was a little intimidating," I admitted.

"I hardly ever sit on it myself," Mr. Davis confided. "I had a designer do the room. She insisted, and since I was paying her for her taste—" He stopped and shook his head. "I can't believe I'm talking about a sofa when Evan—" His voice broke. He tried again. "When Evan is—" But he still couldn't get out the word "dead."

Mr. Davis turned away from us for a moment, and Joe and I exchanged an uneasy look. Grief was radiating out of Evan's dad. Could he be that good an actor? Or if he wasn't acting, could he be so busted up about Evan's death and still be the one who killed him? If *anyone* had killed him. We still didn't have proof that his death wasn't an accident.

"So how do you two know Evan? High school?" asked Mr. Davis.

"No. We, uh, we met Evan at the Haven," Joe explained.

"I don't—what is that?" Mr. Davis said.

"It's a center where homeless teens can stay," I told him.

Mr. Davis's cheeks flushed a deep, painful-looking red. "You can't have known Evan long. Why are you here? Are you looking for some kind of handout? I didn't give it to Evan when he came asking me." Mr. Davis's voice cracked, but he kept on going. "I'm certainly not going to give anything to you two."

"We're not asking for anything," Joe said quickly.

"Then why are you here? The funeral's over. If you wanted to pay your respects, that was the appropriate place to do it," Mr. Davis said.

"We have something that belonged to Evan. We wanted to give it to you." I nodded to Joe, and he handed Mr. Davis the cardboard box with the pictures of Evan in it.

Mr. Davis opened the box, ripping one of the cardboard flaps in his hurry. He pulled out the pictures and let the box fall to the floor. I kept my eyes locked on Evan's father as he flipped through the photos, but his face remained blank.

"I want you out of here," he finally said, his voice low and harsh. "Now! I have no problem calling the cops."

"Evan had this box with him the day he died," I tried to explain. "We thought you should have it, that you'd want to know everything there was to know about that day—about Evan."

"I do know everything there is to know about my son!" yelled Mr. Davis. "I also know when two punks are trying to blackmail me."

I stood up. So did Joe. "That's not why we came here. We came because we care about Evan," I said.

"If you don't get out of here, you're going to get more than you bargained for. I promise you that," Mr. Davis threatened.

"How did it go with Evan's dad?" Lily asked as soon as we'd joined her at a table all the way in the back of the common room.

"He kicked us out," answered Joe, "after he threatened to call the cops—or was it before?" He looked at me.

"I think it was both," I said.

"So that's it? He tells you to go and you just go? Is that how you solved all your cases?" Lily demanded.

I did a room check. Nobody seemed to be paying any attention to us. "Keep it down, okay?" I told Lily.

"Look," Joe said, "we think you could be right about Mr. Davis. We think he might have murdered Evan, or maybe paid someone to do it. But that's only one possibility. Wait, I mean that's only two possibilities. We have to uncover every possible person who could have wanted Evan dead."

"Joe's right," I added. "It's way too soon to focus on just one suspect. That's not the way we solve cases."

"You're wasting your time on anybody but Mr. Davis," Lily insisted. "You didn't see the way he talked to Evan. I did. It was like Mr. Davis hated him. All he cared about was that he might possibly lose the election."

"We're not done with Mr. Davis. I promise," I told Lily. "Okay?"

She didn't answer. Her blue eyes were icy. "Okay?" I repeated.

"Just trust us a little," said Joe.

"Okay." Lily sighed. "At least somebody cares about Evan. Somebody besides me. He was so great. He didn't deserve to die. I want to see his killer pay."

Before Joe or I could answer, Sean came into the

room. "How was your little tea party?" Mark called over to him. "You ready to go upstairs and pack your bags for college with all your new cash?"

"It might take me longer than I thought," Sean answered. "But I'll get there."

"We're all sure you will," a plump woman with silver hair said as she stepped up to him and put her hand on his shoulder.

"I don't know whether that's a polyester dress," Joe said softly. "But I'm thinking that has to be Tess Markham."

The woman raised her voice. "You're all going to get where you want to go. I won't stop until you do."

"What about me, Tess?" whined Nina. "I've been here a lot longer than Sean. How come he got the fancy tea party before I got anything?"

"I'm out of here," Lily said softly. "Hearing about the fund-raiser just makes me think of Evan. He was so happy when he got back from that dinner Tess set up for him." She stood up and headed for the door.

"I have to match the teen I'm presenting with the group I'm presenting to," Tess explained. "I've told you all this before. The tea was for women who are very active in charities that involve animals. I thought they'd respond well to a teen who wanted to be a vet. They were touched by the stories about all the pets Sean has had. And they were impressed by his math and science grades."

They may have been impressed, but from the way Sean was acting, they hadn't donated all that much money.

"Does that answer your question, Nina?" Tess asked.

"I guess," Nina muttered.

"Good. Now, excuse me, everyone, while I say hello to our newest guests." Tess walked over to me and Joe and sat down at our table. "I'm sorry I wasn't here when you arrived. But I know Sandy took care of you. He's the best."

"Definitely," Joe said.

"This is a great place. We're glad we found it," I told her.

"I am too," Tess answered. "I hate to think about kids who don't find the Haven—or someplace like it." She frowned a little, and I wondered if she was thinking of her son. "Not that there actually are any places like the Haven. This is the best center for runaways in the city."

"Take a look at all the awards on her office walls if you don't believe her," called Rosemary.

"I believe!" Joe exclaimed.

Tess laughed. "You're Joe, am I right? And you're Frank."

"How'd you know which of us was which?" I asked.

"I have my methods." She winked. "Sandy described you both. But I need a lot more information than he gave me. Hopes, dreams, aspirations. Tell Tess. You've heard what I can do when I match the right teen with the right people with money. You first, Joe."

"Me. Uh . . ." Joe stared up at the ceiling, thinking.

"Come on. Didn't you ever think about what you wanted to be when you grew up?" Tess teased gently.

"A Major League pitcher," said Joe.

"That might be a little tough as a fund-raising angle. Anything else?" Tess asked.

"A police officer, maybe," Joe answered, and I knew he was thinking of our dad.

"Hmm. A noble calling. But have you thought about law? You should think about it." She glanced at her watch. "Oooh, I'm late for a meeting. But it was great to meet both of you. You have nice manners. I like to see that. And so do the donors." She gave us a little wave as she walked away.

• • • •

That night I couldn't fall asleep. I kept running over the suspects in my head. Tess seemed really cool when we met her today. And it was great the way she got the kids here money for school.

But she was obviously really proud of the Haven. And it seemed like her whole life revolved around it. I wondered how far she'd go to protect its reputation.

What about Sandy? He seemed like he thought Tess was amazing. And she supposedly treated him almost like he was her son. What would Sandy do to protect Tess and the Haven?

My brain felt like it was closing down as I started thinking about Olivia. Photos . . . blackmailing . . .

I couldn't stay awake. I drifted off to the sound of Joe snoring, which he claims he doesn't do.

But it wasn't Joe's snores that woke me up. It was a soft sound—but a sound that didn't seem like it belonged in the dorm in the middle of the night: a clicking. I sat up and squinted into the darkness around me.

I didn't see anything suspicious. Had I heard the door clicking shut? Had someone been sneaking around in the dorm? *It could have been someone heading out to the bathroom*, I told myself.

I started to lie back down, and that's when I saw

it: the ripped sheet taped to the wall between my bed and Joe's. A message had been written across the white cloth in dripping red letters. Blood?

I leaned closer to read the words. "Go home—or die."

10.
THIEF

"Nice love note, guys," Sean said.

"Jealous?" I shot back.

Frank reached out and ran his fingers across the dripping red letters of the word "die."

"I really thought this was written in blood last night," he said.

"Well, it's not like you wear a lot of nail polish. Only on special occasions, am I right?" I asked.

Frank snorted. "Somebody must have used a whole bottle of the stuff to write this." He pulled the sheet off the wall and folded it up. Then we headed out to the hallway where we could talk without an audience.

"Any idea who the somebody could be?" I used my fingers to smooth down my hair. I could feel

I had some intense bed head going on.

" 'Get out or die.' That sounds a little like what Evan's dad said to us yesterday. He said we'd get more than we bargained for," Frank answered.

I did my one-eyebrow raise. "Death is definitely more than I bargained for."

"Yeah," agreed Frank. "It's hard to imagine Mr. Davis sneaking into the Haven in the middle of the night, though. For one thing, if he got caught, it would create the kind of scandal he's trying to avoid."

"We talked about Mr. Davis maybe having hired somebody to kill Evan. Maybe he hired somebody to deliver the warning," I suggested.

"It wouldn't have been hard at all for Tess or Sandy to get into the dorm. But if they did, it would mean that somebody's figured out we aren't just your basic runaways," Frank said.

"I don't think we've given ourselves away," I told him. "Lily's the only one who knows the truth about us. And she wants us to figure out what happened to Evan. She wouldn't be trying to scare us off."

"Olivia's our other big suspect. But I don't think she's figured out we're detectives either," Frank said.

"Not after my masterful performance as a

pickpocket," I agreed. "There's one thing that bugs me about Olivia as a suspect, though. Our theory is that she might have been blackmailing Evan, and he went on the attack."

Frank nodded. "That still makes sense to me."

"Me too," I agreed. "But the timing is really convenient, don't you think?"

"What do you mean?" asked Frank.

"Well, Evan was killed when he was on his way to talk to a reporter about something going on at the Haven," I explained. "If Olivia killed Evan, that means she just happened to prevent him from talking to the reporter—because Olivia wouldn't care if Evan talked to the press about this place."

"It would be a weird coincidence. But those do happen sometimes," Frank said.

"So who else do we have on our suspect list?" I asked.

Joe didn't have time to answer before the shouting started up from downstairs.

"You're not getting away with it!" somebody yelled.

A softer voice murmured a reply.

"I wasn't sure before, but I am now! You're sick!" the first voice shouted. You could hear the raw fury.

"Let's check it out," said Frank. He took the

stairs two at a time. When we hit the downstairs hallway, we saw Mark facing off with Tess.

"There are people I can tell," Mark ranted on. "You think I don't have any power, but you're—"

Tess put her hand on his arm. "Let's talk about this in my office."

Mark pulled away. "Why? You don't want people to hear? I think everybody should. I think—"

"You don't want to say any more out here. Believe me," Tess told him, shooting a glance at me and Frank. "Let's go into my office."

Sandy stepped into the hall. "Problems?" he asked.

"I just want Mark to come into my office for a chat. We have a little situation we need to resolve. Nothing serious," Tess told Sandy.

"Mark, are you going to go discuss whatever the issue is in a calm way?" Sandy asked.

"Fine. But it's not like sitting in your office is going to change anything," Mark told Tess as they started walking toward her office.

"You two need to get dressed for breakfast," Tess called over her shoulder to me and Frank.

"What do you think that was about?" I asked Frank as we headed back upstairs.

"Sounds like Mark's very unhappy with Tess. It kind of sounded like he found out whatever it was that Evan was going to talk to that reporter about," Frank said.

"And Mark decided to go straight to Tess with it," I added.

"I think Mark has just become our best lead to finding out whether Evan was murdered or not," Frank told me.

Frank and I made sure to sit at the same table as Mark at breakfast. He shoveled oatmeal into his mouth in silence, not even looking at anybody else.

"What's your damage?" Lily finally asked him.

"Yeah," Nina said. "We heard you yelling at Tess this a.m. What was up? The only reason anybody should be on her case is her bad fashion sense."

"Nothing," Mark muttered, keeping his gaze on his cereal.

"Nothing? That's bull," Erin told him. "You don't yell loud enough to be heard in the girl's dorm when you're talking about nothing."

"Tess—" Mark hesitated. "Yesterday she told me I could get out of lunch-cooking duty today. Then this morning she tells me she changed her mind."

"Yeah, right," said Lily. Nina and Erin exchanged a *he's so lying* look. Jason grunted in what sounded like agreement.

Was there anyone at the table who didn't think Mark was lying? Who got so bent over something like having to cook lunch? Everybody at the Haven had to do stuff like that.

The kind of stuff Mark was yelling at Tess—"You're not getting away with it"—could apply to Tess going back on her agreement to let Mark skip lunch duty, but it was a real stretch. Mark had sounded practically homicidal when he was shouting that stuff.

Mark shoveled the last few spoonfuls of oatmeal into his mouth. Then, without a word, he got up and stomped toward the kitchen to drop off his bowl.

"I think I'm done too," Frank said, even though his bowl was still half-full.

I took the hint. "Me too."

We both stood up and followed after Mark. "I think we should trail him today," Frank whispered as we crossed the dining hall.

I nodded. "Seems like he knows something we should know."

We dumped our dishes by the sink for the morning cleaning crew to deal with. Then we walked out to the hallway and followed Mark as he headed outside. We were careful to give him a decent head start. We weren't going to find out anything we needed if he knew we were following him.

Mark strode down Twenty-third Street, heading east. There were lots of people heading to work, which gave us some good cover as we trailed him. He took us all the way over to Second Avenue, then hung a right.

Practically every block we passed on Second had a place that sold pizza by the slice. None of them were open. Too early. But that didn't stop my stomach from growling.

"He's going to hear us if your belly gets any louder," Frank said.

"I didn't get to finish breakfast," I protested.

"Hey, wait. Isn't that Olivia up there?" asked Frank as we approached St. Mark's Place.

"Yeah. Looks like Mark sees her too." We watched Mark cut across the street, heading straight toward Olivia. He shoved her up against the wall of yet another pizza place. Then he jerked her backpack off her shoulders.

Faux Hawk guy—whose name we'd found out was Eli—tried to grab it back from him, but Mark elbowed him away. He rummaged through the backpack and pulled out Olivia's camera. He dropped the pack and shook the camera in Olivia's face. I could tell he was shouting at her, but Frank and I were too far away to hear the words.

"He seems as mad at her as he was at Tess," Frank commented.

Mark raised the camera over his head, then slammed it down on the pavement.

"Maybe madder," I said as Mark stomped on the camera with one of his heavy work boots.

Olivia and her crew seemed to have decided to let Mark do whatever he was going to do. They watched as he brought his foot down on the camera again. Then he stormed away.

"We definitely need to find out what that was about," said Frank. "We need to dig up more info about Evan's father, too. The way he went off yesterday—it just made me more suspicious of him."

"Want to split up?" I asked.

"Good idea. You should hang with Olivia. She's already starting to trust you, I think. You sort of proved yourself to her by picking that man's pocket," Frank answered.

I nodded. "I'll wait a little while before I head over there. I don't want anyone to think I might have been following Mark—or even that I saw what just happened."

"I'll head back out to Long Island. I think I'll scope out Mr. Davis's campaign headquarters, see if I can find out anything from the people who are working for him," Frank said.

"I'll meet you at Gray's Papaya at four," I told him.

"Gray's Papaya is nowhere near the Haven," Frank protested.

"I know. But I've been thinking about those Gray's hot dogs since the last time we were here with Mom and Dad," I said.

Frank stared at me. "That was more than four years ago."

"Those were some very good hot dogs," I pointed out.

"Actually, they *were* pretty good. See you there at four." Frank turned and headed for the closest subway station. It was only about a block away.

I went into a tiny Korean grocery store and bought myself a Rice Krispies square. I needed some food in me if I was going to be in top shape while I was observing Olivia. When I finished every marshmallowy bite, I wandered toward Olivia.

Eli and Shay were with her, and a guy I hadn't seen before who looked sort of like a young Jack Black.

"Joe, hey!" Olivia called when she spotted me. "Where's the brother whose name should be Robert?"

"Frank had some stuff to do," I answered as I

joined her group. "What are you guys up to today?"

"The first thing we have to do is get me a new camera," answered Olivia.

"What happened to your old one?" I asked. I was curious whether or not she'd tell me the truth.

"Some psycho grabbed it and smashed it." Olivia swept her hand toward the sidewalk, where pieces of the camera were still scattered.

So I'd gotten a partial truth. Olivia hadn't mentioned she knew the psycho in question. "Why'd somebody do that?" I asked.

"Aw, you haven't been in the city for long, have you, little boy?" Shay asked. "There are crazies all over the place. Once this woman punched me in the chest. Didn't say anything first. I didn't step on her foot or ask her for anything. She just walked up to me and *wham*!"

"Jeez," the Jack Black–looking guy muttered.

"Yeah, Alex, jeez," Shay said, sarcasm dripping off her.

"Don't fight, chicklets," Olivia told them. "Where should we go shopping for my camera?"

"Kmart has an okay selection. And it's only a few blocks away," Shay said.

"Let's hit it." Olivia started walking, and the rest of us fell in around her.

When we reached Kmart we took the escalator

to the second floor, then found the electronics department. "Okay, here's the plan," Olivia said. "Shay and Alex, you stage some kind of distraction. Whatever you think would be fun. And, Joe, when everybody's attention is on those two, you grab me one of those Sony Cyber-shots. Eli and I will run interference if necessary. Got it?"

Alex, Shay, and Eli nodded. I was amazed at how willing they were for Olivia to hand out orders. I guess she took care of them, in her way—like teaching me to pickpocket so I'd have money to eat, and giving me and Frank the tip about the Haven.

But I really did not want to steal a camera—or anything else. I knew I'd worked it out for the man whose wallet I stole to get it back, but the wallet had a name and address inside, so the cops could find the owner, no problem. The camera was a different deal.

"Questions, Joe?" Olivia asked. "The camera's small. You should be able to shove it inside your jacket. Just be casual. Don't bolt as soon as you have it stowed. Take your time, look around. Maybe even buy a little something. A candy bar or whatever. You have money?"

"Yeah," I answered. "But . . . won't the camera have a sensor on it? The alarms will go off as soon as I get to the door."

Shay looked me up and down. "You're in good shape. I bet you can run pretty fast."

Olivia laughed. "Yeah, Joe. Afraid of a little exercise?"

"No. Definitely not," I said quickly. I needed to have some time around Olivia to figure out what the deal between her and Mark was. If I didn't steal the camera, I doubted she'd be very interested in having me in her sight.

"We'll meet up in the Astor Place subway," said Olivia. "Uptown side."

"That's the one with the big black cube near it, right?" I asked.

"Right." She turned to Alex and Shay. "You're up. Make it good."

Alex and Shay walked over to the aisle that was one over from the cameras. "Get ready," Olivia told me.

My heart was doing a drum solo in my chest as I walked over to the display of cameras. I made sure the one Olivia wanted was just a quick grab away.

Even though I wasn't going to steal it. I couldn't.

"I saw you flirting with that redhead!" I heard Shay shout.

"You're so paranoid," Alex yelled back.

The distraction had started.

"I'm not paranoid. Don't try to make me feel like there's something wrong with me when you're the total dog!" Shay shrieked. She was really getting into it.

"What's the problem?" I heard someone else say. "We can't have this kind of commotion in the store."

I figured it had to be a security guard or a clerk talking. This was my shot.

I snatched the camera and shoved in under my coat. I had to. I was sure Olivia was watching.

I walked down the aisle, pretending to browse, but I felt like there was a big blinking sign over my head. A sign that said THIEF! RIGHT HERE! THIEF! with a big arrow pointing down at me, in case anybody didn't get it.

Suddenly I heard Frank's voice in my head. *There's always more than one possible action in every situation.*

My heart rate slowed down a little. I could handle this. I just needed to think. Okay, so I'd proven to Olivia that I was on board. She'd seen me take the camera. I was sure of that.

But if I happened to drop the camera on my way out . . . in a place where a security guard could see me . . . well, that wouldn't be me going against Olivia's plan. It would just be me being clumsy.

I strolled over to the escalators. Perfect. A security guard was coming up on one. He could see me. But he couldn't get to me too fast. There was a lady with a baby strapped to her in one of those baby slings.

I took a deep breath and let the camera slide out from under my coat. When it hit the floor, I saw the guard's head snap toward the sound. "You! Stop right there!" he yelled.

Right. I was going to stop right there and let him call the cops. I raced around to the down escalator. Jammed with people. But I didn't have time to look for an alternate route. I jumped on.

"Carl. Stop that kid in the tan jacket," I heard the security guard yell from above me.

A second later I saw another security guard appear at the bottom of the escalator. He grinned at me. He could see I was trapped. There were a bunch of people behind me now too. The escalator was going to drop me at the guard's feet.

Unless . . . I looked over the edge of the escalator rail, estimating the distance to the ground. It was a drop. But I thought I could take it.

I swung myself over the railing and shoved off. Wind rushed against my face as I fell. I landed hard on one knee, but I ignored the bolts of pain. I shoved myself to my feet and ran.

The pounding footfalls of the guard were right behind me. But I really wasn't afraid of a little exercise. I put on the speed, my eyes locked on the big sliding doors of the exit. Just a little farther, just a little.

And I was through. I didn't know if the guard would come after me or not. I didn't slow down to find out. I dodged around the other people on the sidewalk. When I spotted the black cube, I finally let myself take a look behind me. No guard.

I still didn't ease up. I ran over to the stairs leading to the subway station and flew down them.

Safe. I was safe. Unless Olivia figured out I'd dropped the camera on purpose.

FRANK

11.
DEAD

I knew what Joe would tell me to do in this situation—flirt.

The twentyish girl with the curly black hair manning a bank of phones in Mr. Davis's campaign headquarters was looking at me. But I wasn't sure if it was in an interested way. Or in a *what are you doing here* way.

I heard Joe's voice in my head. *Smile, dummy.*

I smiled. The girl smiled back. The smile created dimples in both cheeks. *I guess I could say something about the dimples*, I thought. *That was sort of flirty—unless it was sort of pathetic.*

I couldn't just stand there staring at her, so I walked over. "I like your dimples," I said.

It definitely sounded pathetic coming out of my

mouth. And I felt my face get hot. *I'd better not be blushing*, I thought.

"Thanks. I've had them my whole life," the girl answered. "So what can I do for you? I'm Nora, by the way."

"Here's the deal. We're doing this project in social studies where we're supposed to find out about a profession we're interested in." It was the best thing I could think of. But the project sounded more like something you'd do in the fourth grade than in high school.

"And you're interested in being a volunteer phone answerer for a mayoral candidate?" Nora teased. "It *is* very exciting. But I wouldn't exactly call it a profession."

"I was thinking more of a politician. I don't really know much of what the day-to-day job is. But I think it's probably one of the best careers to have if you really want to make an impact on the world," I told her.

"I'm sure Mr. Davis would be happy to take a few minutes to talk to you, but he's not here right now," Nora said. "Let's go into his office and check his appointment book. He has to have a free spot somewhere."

Score! I thought. Mr. Davis's appointment book was exactly what I needed. I wanted to find out where he was when Evan was killed.

Nora stood up and I followed her into a little office. This was clearly where Mr. Davis really lived. Unlike his perfect living room, his office was cluttered. There were food wrappers on the desk, stacks of papers on both of the chairs in front of the desk, and a map of Lake Ronkonkoma on the wall with red and blue thumbtacks all over it. I was thinking they represented Republican and Democrat areas.

"It's always almost impossible to find anything in here," Nora complained as she rooted around on the desktop. "Here it is." She pulled an appointment book out from under a stack of magazines and flipped it open. "Mr. Davis puts everything in here. He hasn't quite entered the electronic age. No Blackberry or anything like that."

She scanned the book. "Wow, he's truly over-scheduled. But how about next Tuesday? Around lunchtime? He doesn't have anything written down, which means he'll be eating right there." She pointed to the chair in behind the desk.

"Uh, actually, this project, it's due tomorrow. I kind of procrastinated a little bit," I said.

Nora shook her finger at me. "Too busy having fun, I bet."

"Yeah, I guess," I admitted.

"Just don't let it drag your grade point average down. It gets harder to get into a good college every year. I barely squeaked into Hunter," said Nora. "So do you have a second choice to do your project on? I can still tell you all about being a volunteer phone answerer."

"We had to sign up for the career when the project was assigned. I already told my teacher I was doing politician," I answered. "Do you think it would be okay if I just flipped through the appointment book, maybe? That would give me some idea of the kind of thing Mr. Davis spends his time doing. I can probably fake the rest."

She hesitated. I smiled at her. She smiled back. "All right, but only a quick look, okay? The head of us volunteers will be back any minute. I'm not sure if she'd be okay with it."

"Five minutes, tops," I promised. "You should get back to your phones. I don't want you to get in trouble for abandoning them to help me."

"Yeah, I have to get back out there. I'm getting college credit for this. I can't slack." She hurried out of the office, shutting the door behind her.

I immediately flipped back in the appointment book to the day Evan died. Mr. Davis was supposed to have given a speech at the Kiwanis Club at lunch. Evan had died at about one o'clock. That meant if Mr. Davis had shown up as scheduled, he couldn't have killed Evan.

Still, that didn't mean he couldn't have paid somebody to do it—maybe whoever left me and Joe that threat.

I'd been in the office by myself for only a couple of minutes. I decided I should be able to take a few more without Nora checking on me. I sat down in front of the computer and logged on. I'd seen a Bank of America a few blocks from the campaign headquarters. And the center was pretty close to Mr. Davis's house.

The odds seemed good that he had an account there. People usually go to the nearest bank. I quickly found the Bank of America site. Now the tricky part. I needed Mr. Davis's ID and password to log on.

I remembered my dad giving Aunt Trudy a hard time for just using her first and last name as her ID on some online site. Mr. Davis wasn't Mr. Electronics. Maybe he didn't think too much about computer security.

I typed in martindavis for the ID. Now the password. Mr. Davis had little notes to himself on Post-its all over the desk. It didn't seem like he was the kind of guy to keep things in his head.

I scanned the desk, looking for anything that seemed like a password. I saw a short grocery list, the name and author of a book. There was one Post-it that just had the word "shirts" on it.

I thought that was probably to remind him to get his dry cleaning or something, but I typed it in anyway. Nope. No go.

But as I'd typed, the keyboard had slid forward a little, revealing . . . bingo. A Post-it with "balloon17" on it. That sounded very password. I typed it in. Another bingo.

If Mr. Davis had hired somebody to kill Evan, he would have needed to pay out a big chunk of money. I scrolled through his checking account entries for the past three months. Then his savings account info. No withdrawals or checks for anywhere near what it would take to have somebody killed.

It looked like Mr. Davis was clean.

No, there was an assumption in there. I reminded myself that just because Mr. Davis had an appointment in his calendar didn't mean he'd kept it.

I figured Nora could help me out with this, too. I walked out of the office and over to her desk. "Did you get enough to scrape by on your project?" she asked.

"I think so," I answered. "There was one thing I didn't get. Mr. Davis was scheduled to give a speech at the Kiwanis Club. I don't even know what a Kiwanis is."

"I'm not exactly sure myself," Nora admitted. "And I was at that speech! It's some kind of community service organization or something like that."

"You were there?" I asked.

"Yeah. The volunteers take turns going to events with Mr. D. Just in case he needs anything. He was amazing. He got a standing O," Nora said.

He's also got an airtight alibi, I thought.

"So that's one suspect off our list," I told Joe as we walked toward the Haven. We were both stuffed full of Gray's Papaya hot dogs.

"That's a good day's work," Joe said. "Unlike mine. I didn't find out any details about why Mark was so angry at Olivia. I didn't find out any new info about Mark at all."

"You managed to keep Olivia as a contact, though," I told him, "without stealing anything. That's not too shabby. I think Olivia might really have a piece to this puzzle. I'm not sure what it—"

The sound of Joe drawing in a sharp breath stopped me. "What?" I asked.

Then I saw what he'd seen. Halfway down the block, a stretcher was being wheeled out of the Haven. The body on the stretcher was completely draped in a white sheet.

Dead.

12.

THE MORGUE

Frank and I pounded down the pavement to the Haven. "What happened?" I called.

It was Lily who answered. "Mark overdosed," she said, so softly I almost couldn't hear her.

"He was doing so good, too. He'd been going to a Narcotics Anonymous meeting every day for months," Erin added. She gave a limp, helpless shrug.

"He was an addict. Addicts relapse," Josh told her.

I heard the doors of the paramedics' van slam. I turned my head in time to see the van pull away and disappear around the corner. And that was it. Mark was gone. None of us would ever see him again.

I kept staring down the street, like I expected the van to pull up in reverse and Mark to jump out, alive and well. "An overdose. Man."

"Have you thought about the timing? It's the definition of convenient," Frank noted when we were out of earshot from the others.

I forced myself to start thinking like a detective. "Ultraconvenient, because he'd just had major fights with two of our main suspects for killing Evan."

Frank pulled in a deep breath. I knew what he was thinking. I was thinking the same thing myself. "You think maybe somebody murdered Mark, too? And made it look like he OD'd?" I asked.

"I absolutely think we have to investigate the possibility," my brother answered.

"Maybe we split up again," I suggested. "Try to talk to as many people as possible. Find out who found the body and all that."

"I think there's something we should do first," said Frank. "I think we need to make a trip to the morgue."

"The log book said Mark's corpse should be in room B," Frank said. "I want to get a look at the coroner's notes. They should be in there too." We quickly walked down the cracked linoleum of the morgue building. A quick search on the Internet had told us where bodies of victims from the Haven's police precinct were brought. We thought we'd waited long enough for the coroner to have done his stuff.

"That's room A," I pointed out. "So after a series of calculations, I hypothesize that the next one is room B." My jokes get a little stupider when I'm nervous. And I admit, being in the morgue was minorly creeping me out. I felt like I was in the beginning of a zombie movie or something.

"Your hypothesis is correct." Frank stopped in front of the next door, which was labeled ROOM B.

"So what are the coroner's hours?" I asked softly. "You think anyone's in there? Anyone alive, I mean." And the bad jokes keep on coming.

"I'm going to open the door a little. Try and get a look inside," Frank instructed.

He cracked the door and I pressed one eye against the narrow opening. I saw the end of several metal tables. A big metal ventilation hood near a double sink. A couple of scales. No people, corpse or animate.

"We're clear," I said.

Frank swung the door open wide and we ducked inside. "We need to find the paperwork on Mark," he told me.

I spotted a clipboard on one of the metal tables. I hurried over and picked it up, then f lipped through the pages. "Got it."

Frank looked over my shoulder as I started to read. "There were abrasions on his knuckles," he pointed out. "Sounds like he was doing some fighting today."

"Abrasions on the roof of his mouth, too," I commented. "And bruises around his lips."

"So maybe somebody forced the pills on him," said Frank.

"Scraping up the inside of his mouth and bruising him in the process," I agreed.

"And he got his knuckles messed up fighting them off," Frank guessed. "He—"

"Wait. I think I hear someone coming," I interrupted. We both froze, listening.

"You're right. We can't get caught in here," Frank whispered.

I put the clipboard back on the table. My eyes swept over the room, looking for a hiding place. "The drawers," I said, as in, the big metal drawers where the bodies are stored.

I slid open the closest one. Empty. I sucked in a deep breath and climbed in. I slid the door almost all the way closed, leaving a crack for air. *You've got plenty of O$_2$*, I told myself. *Plenty*.

The metal slab under my body was cold, and the coldness seeped through my clothes. Through my skin. Until it felt like my bones were sticks of ice.

I tried to concentrate on the sounds in the room. Voices. A thump. Wheels. But my thoughts kept circling around what this drawer was used for. Who had been in it before me. I admit it, I was freaking myself out a little.

Sounds, I told myself. *Focus on the sounds*. But there weren't any. I listened harder. I didn't hear any voices or movement out there.

I braced my hands on the metal walls and slid the drawer open. I was right. The room was empty. I scrambled down to the floor and pulled open Frank's drawer. Seeing him lying there was almost as freaky as being stretched out in one of the drawers myself.

"So are we done here?" I asked Frank as he climbed free.

"I just want to take another fast look at the coroner's notes. I want to make sure we haven't missed anything," Frank told me. He crossed the room and grabbed the clipboard. "The report's gone."

"Just his?" I asked.

"I think so. The stack of forms doesn't seem much thinner."

"Whoever just came in must have taken it," I said.

"I don't like this," Frank told me.

"Me either. Let's try to catch up with them. That paper is important evidence. We don't want it going anywhere it shouldn't," I said.

"They can't have gotten too far," Frank reasoned. We hurried to the door. Took a quick look out to make sure the hallway was empty and that no one would see us coming out of the morgue. The coast was clear. We stepped out of the room.

"Hold up," I said quietly. "I think I hear metal wheels. Hear that squeaking?"

"Yeah. It's coming from down there," Frank answered. We raced after the sound. When we rounded the corner at the end of the hall, we saw two men wheeling a gurney. A sheet-covered body lay on top.

I looked at Frank. "You think?" I asked softly.

"One way to find out," he whispered.

We hung back and watched as the men rolled the gurney out a door leading to a parking lot. Then we followed. Through a small, square window crisscrossed with wires, we saw the men load the gurney into a truck.

"Do they usually move bodies around in trucks?"

"There doesn't seem to be much that's usual in this situation," Frank replied. "That body should be part of a police investigation. There hasn't been enough time for that."

"Could they be moving him to another morgue, you think?" I asked as the men got into the cab of the truck.

"It's not like this one is overcrowded or anything," Frank said. "There were empty drawers—as we both know. Feel like taking a little ride?"

"You got it," I answered. We left the building and ran over to the truck, keeping low to the ground. I tried to open the back door of the truck—locked, of course.

But locked doors aren't really a problem if you've been trained by ATAC. Frank pulled a lock pick out of his jacket pocket. The truck's engine rolled over as he started working the lock.

Frank got the door open just in time for us to jump on board as the truck began to move out of the parking lot. He clicked the door shut behind us.

I pulled out my key chain. It had a tiny but super powerful flashlight on the end. I clicked it on, and the back of the truck was flooded with light.

"This truck definitely isn't meant to transport bodies," Frank commented. It was true. Most of the space was jammed with furniture and boxes.

The gurney looked bizarre among what looked like the contents of a regular moving van.

"We might as well make sure this is who we think it is," I said. I pulled back the sheet. It was Mark. I quickly covered his face again.

"Here are the coroner's notes," Frank said, touching a sheet of paper that was stuck halfway under the body. He shook his head. "Why do I feel like we're missing something?"

I lifted the part of the sheet that was over Mark's feet. "It's not that we're missing something," I pointed out. "It's that something's missing. There's no ID."

"That's it!" Frank exclaimed. "That's what was bugging me. No toe tag."

The truck started moving faster. We were clearly out of the stop-and-go traffic of Manhattan and on a freeway.

"Where do you think they're taking the body? And us?" I asked.

Frank shook his head. "I don't know. But I have a feeing it's no place we want to be."

13.
POTTER'S FIELD

The truck pulled to a stop. The rumble of the engine died. "Help me move that couch out a little," I said to Joe. "I think we can both squeeze behind it. Who knows what the goons driving the truck would do if they found us back here."

"I definitely don't want to end up back in a morgue drawer today—or pretty much ever," Joe stated.

We shoved the couch out and scrambled behind it about two seconds before the back doors of the truck swung open. I tried not to even breathe as I heard the gurney being unloaded.

As soon as the doors slammed closed, I sucked in a lungful of air. "Let's see where we ended up," I told Joe. We waited five minutes—five minutes that felt like twenty—so we wouldn't run into the guys from the front of the truck. Then Joe and I climbed out.

"Stay back," Joe whispered. "The guys are still in sight."

I spotted them about a hundred feet away, standing on a small wooden pier that jutted out into what I assumed was the Long Island Sound. We definitely weren't in Manhattan anymore.

As we watched, using the truck as cover, the men loaded Mark's body into an oyster boat. Within minutes, the boat was heading across the water, the motor the only sound along the deserted stretch of beach.

"Let's check the front of the truck," suggested Joe. "See if we can find out who we're dealing with."

"Good idea." We trotted around to the front of the truck and got in. Joe started going through the glove compartment. I spotted a clipboard on the floor and picked it up.

"Tess," Joe burst out.

"What?" I exclaimed.

He waved a check in my face. "Made out to the Move It Moving Company, and signed by Tess."

I checked out the papers on the clipboard. "I've got a Tess signature too. This is paperwork from the morgue. It's instructions to have Mark's body transported to his family in D.C. Tess signed it," I explained.

"They definitely aren't heading toward D.C.," Joe commented.

I looked out the window. The boat was heading toward a small island. "Hart Island," I burst out.

"What?"

"Hart Island. I think that's where they're headed." I pointed out another island in the Sound. "That's the Stepping Stone Lighthouse over there. Hart Island is close to that. And the island the boat is heading to is small. It has to be Hart. They're going to bury the body in potter's field."

"Catch me up. I've never even heard of Hart Island," said Joe.

"Chet did a report about Rikers Island for history. He said one of the things the inmates had to do was bury bodies in the potter's field on Hart Island. It's where the city buries bodies no one claims.

"Tess paid them to dispose of the body and the coroner's notes. No body. No notes. No evidence," I said.

"And Tess wanted no evidence, because she killed Mark," Joe added. "I think Mark found out whatever Evan discovered about the Haven. That's what he was fighting with Tess about. She killed him so he couldn't tell—just like she killed Evan!"

"Probably," I agreed. "But we need proof."

I opened my eyes at exactly three a.m. It's a thing I can do. When I'm falling asleep, I repeat the time I want to wake up over and over in my head. And it always works, even when I'm really tired. And I was. That pier on the Long Island Sound was in the middle of nowhere. Joe and I'd had to walk more than five miles before we found a town with a bus that would take us back to the city.

I got out of bed and shook Joe by the shoulder. "Wake up," I whispered. He didn't even roll over. At home, Aunt Trudy sometimes has to pour cold water over his head to get him up in the morning.

"Joe, wake up," I whispered again. I shook him harder.

"It's Frank's turn to take out the garbage," he muttered, eyes still closed. I think ATAC should train us how to wake up quickly. If they had a program like that I'd sign Joe up yesterday.

"I'm going down to the kitchen. I'm not even going to bother with water. I'm getting ice cubes," I threatened, speaking directly into Joe's ear. I didn't want to wake any of the other guys up.

Joe sat up fast. "I'm awake. What time is it?"

"It's time," I told him.

He got out of bed and we crept downstairs to Tess's office. It was locked. But, like I said, that's never a problem. I pulled out the lock pick. A couple of flicks of the wrist, and we were in.

Joe and I started searching the office. I took the desk, feeling like I was back at Mr. Davis's campaign headquarters. You do a lot of grunt work as a detective—a lot of watching, a lot of searching through papers.

The contents of Tess's desk were pretty ordinary: business cards; paper clips—colored ones, not regular metal; rubber bands—also colored; and a stack of the Haven letterhead. I spun the desk chair around and pulled open the top drawer of her filing cabinet. It was filled with tax records.

I started flipping through. "Wow, Tess makes, like, no money," I told Joe. I did a fast calculation. "She pays herself just about minimum wage."

"Well, we already knew she doesn't spend money on clothes, at least according to Karen," Joe commented as he checked behind the books on Tess's shelves.

I kept flipping through the tax forms. No major changes in the amount of money Tess brought in from year to year. But I did notice something strange.

"Tess didn't claim any dependents," I said. "Which makes sense from the time her son ran away. But even before that, she didn't put him down on her tax forms." I checked a few more years. "She's never claimed him."

"That's weird. Mom always says one of the reasons she's glad she had children is because of the tax break," Joe said.

I frowned. "It's really weird. But it doesn't seem like it connects to Evan or Mark getting killed."

"Oh, score!" Joe said. "Tess has a floor safe. If there's anything she doesn't want anybody to see, it's going to be in there."

I knelt down by the safe next to Joe. "Do you remember the tryout combination for this puppy?" he asked.

"Three-seven-three. But I bet Tess is too smart not to have changed it," I answered. All safes arrive from the manufacturer with a temporary combination in place. It's amazing how many people who shell out big bucks for the security of a safe don't bother to ever reset the combination. All safecrackers know the tryout codes for all the major safe companies.

Joe entered the combination. "You're right. She's a smartie. I guess we'll have to do it the hard way."

"The hard, long way," I said. Cracking a safe isn't like in the movies. You don't just stick your ear to the door and twiddle the knob a little to open the door. Well, actually you mostly do. But it takes a lot longer than the thirty seconds it does on screen.

"I'll start us out." Joe started slowly turning the knob of the dial lock, listening intently. He was trying to figure out the contact points.

You have to be able to picture the inside of a lock to get what that means. There's a spindle that runs from the knob through several wheels, one wheel for each number of the combination. Each of these wheels has a small metal tab sticking out of it. Each wheel also has a notch cut into it. The spindle ends in a drive cam. The drive cam has a drive pin attached to it.

 JOE

Joe here. You don't really have to know all this stuff. You just have to know I'm picking the lock of the safe.

 FRANK

Frank here. This is my section. And I'm describing

the inside of a lock because you can't understand how a safe is cracked if you can't picture the inner workings.

So anyway, when you turn the knob of the safe, the spindle turns the drive cam. As the drive cam turns, the drive pin moves along the closest wheel until it hits the metal tab on the wheel. The tabs are called wheel flies, if you want to get technical about it. When the pin hits the wheel fly, the wheel starts to turn too.

Then the wheel fly on that wheel—the one closest to the drive cam—hits the wheel fly on next wheel. That wheel starts to turn too. This keeps happening until all the wheels in the lock are turning.

When you dial in the right combination the notches on all the wheels end up on top. This row of lined-up notches makes a long, straight gap. The metal bar that has been keeping the safe door from opening falls into the gap. And there you go. Open safe.

Basically, you use the sound the pin makes on the wheels to figure out the combination. First you have to figure out what the lock's contact area is. I need to tell you a little more about the drive cam so you can understand this part. The drive cam also has a notch in it. The notch—

JOE

Joe here. Really, Frank. I'm begging you. It took us two days to learn how to crack a safe. You can't explain it all. Just say I got the safe open. Which, by the way, I did.

FRANK

Frank here. Okay, okay. So Joe got the safe open. It took a couple of hours, because the process is complicated and it requires a lot of explanation to really understand it.

"It's all files," Joe said, reaching inside the safe.

He handed half of the files to me. I flipped through, looking for Evan's or Mark's name.

"I got Evan's," Joe told me.

I leaned in to look as he opened it. The file held copies of all the photos that were in Evan's box, each carefully preserved in a plastic sleeve. "Nothing else in there?" I asked.

"Just one sheet of paper with Evan's contact info on it. Really detailed. Address. Phone. Parents' work numbers. Parents' e-mail addresses," Joe said.

"Why would she have that info?" I asked. "Sandy

didn't make us give him any of that stuff when we came in. He knew we might not stay if he did."

"She had Mark's home address, too, remember? It was on that paperwork we found in the truck—the forms Tess signed," Joe pointed out.

I opened the top file on my stack. It had photos and contact information too. Photos of a teenage girl I'd never seen before. The pictures were a lot like Evan's. They showed the girl begging, picking pockets, shoplifting. "This isn't what I was expecting," I admitted. "This is what I'd expect to see in Olivia's safe—if Olivia had a room to put a safe in."

"There's definitely an Olivia connection going on," Joe said. "I just found Sean's file. Same kind of pics as the others, except Shay and Eli are in one of them."

"Mark has a file too. I wonder if Tess showed it to him when she pulled him into her office the other day," I added.

"She might have used the photos to threaten him to keep quiet about what he found out. He was screaming at her, she brought him into the office, and something shut him up," said Joe.

"This is head-exploding. All these pictures," I said. I glanced at the clock over Tess's desk. It was almost five. "We need to clear out of here."

"Yeah, Tess pretty much lives here," Joe said.

"She's working all the time. She seems so great, running this place, getting the scholarships. I just don't get what Evan and Mark could have found out that Tess would be willing to kill to keep secret."

"Sandy is usually here early too. Who knows when he'll come down here and head to his office? And the breakfast-making crew is going to be up soon," I reminded Joe. "We need to get this stuff back in the safe. But I want to write down the names of everyone who has a file."

Joe grabbed a blank sheet of paper off Tess's desk. "You write, I'll read." He started listing off the names. I wrote them down as quickly as possible.

"Is that it?" I asked when Joe hesitated.

"No," he told me.

"Who's next?" I asked.

"Me." He held out a picture. Looking at it was like a punch to the gut. It showed Joe picking the pocket of the man with the hat in Washington Square Park.

We both stared at the photo for a long moment. "Let's keep going," Joe finally said. He read off the names from the last three files. Then he returned them to the safe, shut the door, and twirled the knob of the lock.

"Whatever Olivia has going with Tess, they work

fast," I commented as we headed back upstairs to the boys' dorm.

"I don't get what Tess would want with those pictures," Joe said. "They're perfect to use for blackmail. But why would she be thinking she'd need to blackmail anybody here? Not for money, that's for sure."

"Maybe it was just kind of an insurance policy. Maybe she thought someday one of the kids here would find out what she was doing, and she'd want the pictures to use to keep them quiet. That's what we're thinking she did with Mark. Maybe she tried it with Evan, too. But he didn't back down. And I guess Mark didn't either. She might have shut him up for a little while after she had her 'talk' with him in her office. But he clearly wasn't willing to let her get away with whatever's going on." I opened the door. "Let's try to get a little sleep before breakfast. It'll help us think better."

Joe nodded as we quietly walked over to our beds. As I stretched out on mine, I felt something lumpy. I reached under my back and pulled out a doll—a dark-haired boy doll.

Its eyes were white Xs. Blood dripped from its mouth.

14.
THREATS

I held my own doll up so Frank could see it. It was the same as his—except it was a little cuter and had blond hair, which makes sense, because clearly it was supposed to be me. I ran my finger over the blood spilling from the doll's mouth.

Frank's gaze moved to the wall behind our beds. Even in the darkness I could read the dripping red words of the new message: "This is you—unless you leave."

"Somebody really wants us gone," Frank whispered. "That's gotta mean we're getting close to the truth."

"Yeah," I whispered back. "We're—"

I saw a flash of movement out of the corner of my eye. I jerked my head in that direction. A figure moved through the shadows at the far end of the room, heading for the door.

I leaped out of bed and raced toward the figure. Frank right behind me. We weren't going to let whoever had been threatening us get away.

The person was fast, but we were fast too. We tore down the hallway. Then down the stairs. I tackled the figure just as we hit the first floor. I couldn't believe who it was when I stared down at the face.

"Lily!" I burst out.

I scrambled to my feet. Frank helped Lily up, keeping a grip on her arm. "We need to talk," he told her. He pulled her into the empty common room. I shut the door behind us and hit the lights. I could see red splotches of nail polish on her hands, but I still found it hard to believe she'd been the one who left us those messages, and those dolls.

"What's going on, Lily?" asked Frank.

"Why didn't you believe me when I told you Evan's father killed him? Why did you break into Tess's office? Why?" she cried.

"You don't get to ask the questions right now," I told her. "Not until you tell us why you've been threatening us."

"Right! What's your connection to Evan's death, Lily? What are you so afraid we're going to find out?" Frank asked.

"I would never have hurt Evan. I loved him. Have you guys even listened to anything I've said?" Lily pressed her hands over her face and shook her head.

"I don't buy it," I said. "If you loved him, you'd want us here. You'd want us to find out if someone killed him."

Lily jerked her hands down. Her eyes blazed as she stared at Frank and me. "I don't want you to die, okay? It won't bring Evan back."

"Die?" Frank repeated.

"Yes, die. As in dead. Because that's what going to happen if you two stay here, digging at things. You're going to get killed. Just like Evan. And now Mark. He found out whatever Evan did. I know it. And he got killed for it too," Lily insisted. "But it's not too late for you yet. Just go. Go back home to Bayport and help somebody track down a lost kitten or something. Don't try to find out what's going on here."

"So . . . what? You left us those notes and the dolls because you were trying to protect us?" I asked.

Lily let out her breath in a long sigh. "I don't understand how you guys are these famous local detectives. You're both incredibly stupid."

"You never thought Evan's father killed Evan, did

you?" Frank asked, his eyes locked on Lily's face.

"I just wanted to get you away from here," Lily admitted. "I figured you'd be out in Long Island for days, doing a stakeout or whatever. And it's not like you'd end up blaming Mr. Davis for something he didn't do. You wouldn't get proof, and you're all about getting proof."

"Let's sit down," Frank suggested.

"Yeah. It seems like this is going to take a while," I agreed. I sat in one of the armchairs. Frank and Lily sat on the sofa across from me. "So you didn't think Evan's dad had anything to do with his death?"

"You should have seen Mr. Davis at Evan's funeral. I was there—just in the back." She gave a harsh laugh. "It's not like I was invited. Anyway, Evan's dad, you could tell he was torn apart. And he made this speech about how his son would still be alive if he had been a better father. He cried. It was horrible. I felt so bad for him—even after he'd been so harsh to Evan that day we went to his house."

"You knew he was innocent even before the funeral, though, didn't you? You knew who killed Evan as soon as it happened. Am I right?" asked Frank.

"You need to drop it, okay? You need to go

home," Lily urged. "Just walk out the door right now and never come back."

"We can take care of ourselves," I told her. "We're not leaving until we have absolute proof of who killed Evan."

I didn't mention Tess. Neither did Joe. We wanted to hear what Lily had to say without putting any ideas into her head.

"We could really use your help," Frank said. "You know things about Evan that no one else does."

"I don't want anyone else to die. I couldn't take it," she said. Her face was so pale, especially next to her black hair.

"We don't want anyone else to die either," I stated. "We can stop that from happening. Together. Just tell us what you know, Lily. Who is it you've been trying to protect us from?"

"Tess," she said. "Tess killed Evan. And Mark. I'm sure of it."

"Why?" Frank asked. "Why did Tess do it?"

"I don't know. I keep trying to figure it out, but nothing makes sense," Lily replied. "All I know is that Evan told me Tess had betrayed him. He was furious with her. He said he was going to bring her down. He said he had a plan—that was the day he died. He told me he had a plan and that he'd tell me everything when he got back. But he never came back. Mark was Evan's closest friend—besides me. He must have started snooping around, and then . . ." She closed her eyes for a minute.

"We know that Evan had an appointment with a reporter named Gwen Anderson that day," I said. "We think he was going to tell her something about the Haven, probably something to do with Tess. But we don't know what."

"So you think Tess killed him too?" Lily asked.

"Yeah," Frank said. "We found out that she had Mark's body taken from the morgue and buried in an anonymous grave where no one would find him. That makes her look pretty guilty. She didn't want his death investigated."

"But we don't have proof," I added, sounding like my brother for a minute.

"We think one of these people might be able to help us with that." Frank pulled the list of names from Tess's files out of his pajama pocket. He handed it to Lily. "Do you know any of them?"

Lily studied the list. "I never actually met any of them. Well, except Joe, of course. But I heard Tess got this one girl, Emma Cassidy, a scholarship to go to Parsons and learn to be a fashion designer. And supposedly she got Philip Stevenson money to go to Harvard. All four years. People still talk about that sometimes."

Frank took the list back. "I have one other question for you. If you think Tess killed Evan—"

"I know she did," Lily interrupted.

"Then why are you still at the Haven?" Frank finished.

Good question. It really didn't make sense that Lily was living here.

"I don't have anywhere else to go. I don't have any cash. I couldn't pay rent on any job I could get. I didn't even graduate high school," Lily admitted.

"There's no chance you could go home?" I asked.

Lily shook her head. "My mom and dad decided to separate. And it's like my mom went nuts. She had to know where I was and what I was doing every second. She even put one of those teddy bears with a camera inside it in my bedroom. I figured if she was going to spy on me, I'd give her something she definitely wouldn't want to see." Lily closed her eyes for a long moment. "It was stupid of me. We ended up having this monster fight. She said she never wanted to see my face again. So I left. What else was I supposed to do?"

"You were fighting. People always say stuff they don't mean when they fight," Frank said.

"She meant it," Lily insisted. "If she couldn't

control every single move I made, she didn't want to have anything to do with me."

"What about going to a different shelter?" I wanted to know.

"I went to another one before I got here. There was a knife fight in the middle of the night," Lily answered. "I was so happy I found this place. It seemed so safe. And I thought Tess was awesome. Pretty stupid, huh?"

"It doesn't seem stupid to me," Frank told her.

"I'm doing this receptionist training program. Sandy got it set up with the people at Kelly Services— the temp agency. When I finish, I should be able to get a job that will pay enough for me to get out of here. But until then, this seems like the best place to live. I just have to keep my head down, stay out of Tess's way. . . ."

She stood up. "I need to go get dressed. I have kitchen duty this morning." She started to the door, then turned back to face us. "I'm sorry I left those signs for you. And the dolls. But I was afraid of what would happen to you. I still am. I still think you should get out of here—before you end up like Evan and Mark."

15.
WHERE'S THE MONEY?

Parsons wasn't too far from the Haven, so we decided to walk over there. We needed to talk to Emma Cassidy. We thought she could be the link we needed to figure out why Tess had all those photos Olivia had taken in her office.

I knew I should be reviewing the case. But I was distracted. "I keep thinking about Lily," I admitted to Joe.

"Me too," said Joe. "She really put in a lot of effort trying to save our necks."

"Yeah. But the part I was thinking about was how she feels like she has to stay at the Haven. Like she has no choice." Thinking about never being able to go home—it made my brain freeze up. I couldn't even really imagine it.

"There's gotta be someplace else she can go. Someplace that's not run by a homicidal maniac," Joe reasoned. "Where there aren't any knife fights. And where she doesn't have to sleep outside—in November."

"We'll have to work on that. . . ."

"As soon as we get the proof we need to close Evan's case. And Mark's," Joe finished for me. "That's Parsons over there. I recognize it from *Project Runway*."

I raised my eyebrows. Both of them.

"It was on in the common room, remember?" he said as we crossed the street and headed inside. We passed glass cases with clothes—some of them pretty weird—on display as we looked for the administration office.

It wasn't too hard to find. A guy wearing a shirt with these puffy flowers on it looked up from the front desk as we stepped inside. "How can I help you?" he asked.

"We were wondering if there's a student directory we could look at," I answered.

"You look a little on the young side to be students here," the guy commented.

"We're not. But my brother's girlfriend goes here. He likes older women," Joe said. "He wants to surprise her."

The guy looked us up and down, and I suddenly remembered how grubby we were, in our runaway teen gear. "We came on the bus from Ohio," I told him. "I guess maybe I should have grabbed a shower before I showed up here. But I was just, um, so excited to see Emma."

"Don't you have her home address?" the guy asked.

"She's not at home. We went there first. We thought maybe we could get her schedule so my brother could surprise her between classes," Joe explained. "Nice fleurchons, by the way."

The guy ran his fingers over one of the puffy flowers. "Thanks. I made them myself."

"Do you go here?" asked Joe.

"This is my last year," the guy answered.

"Emma just started this year. Emma Cassidy. It's the first time she and my brother have been separated." Joe was on a roll. I just let him go. "That's why we were on a bus so long. He had to see her. So can we find out where she is right now?"

"It's against the rules," said the guy. "But I don't want to stand in the way of true love. Just give me a minute." He disappeared into one of the inner offices.

"Fleurchons?" I mouthed at Joe.

"Hey, he's doing it, right?" Joe whispered.

"I think it was the fleurchon compliment that pushed him over the edge. I might start watching *Project Runway* routinely. It's already been useful twice today."

"Emma Cassidy, you said, right?" Fleurchon Guy asked, coming back to the front desk.

"Yes," I answered.

"Any weird spelling or anything?"

"No, just the usual." I spelled out Cassidy for him.

Fleurchon Guy frowned. "I don't know how to tell you this, but your girlfriend isn't here."

"You mean she doesn't have any classes today?" Joe asked.

"I mean that she's never been registered at this school," Fleurchon Guy stated. He looked over at me. "Sorry, dude. Girls lie. It's just a fact."

"Thanks for trying," I told him as Joe and I headed for the door.

I pulled out my cell and punched in 411.

"Who are you calling?" asked Joe.

I held up one finger as I asked the operator for the number of the Harvard admissions office. I chose the option of having the number dialed for me. ATAC can afford it.

"Hello, I'm Frank Hardy over at admissions for Columbia," I said when a woman in Harvard's undergraduate admissions office picked up. "One of your students, Philip Stevenson, is applying for graduate school here and I wanted to have his transcripts sent over."

The woman put me on hold.

"Nice," Joe said.

"It was no fleurchon, but I think it worked," I answered.

After a minute or two of classical music, the woman picked back up. "I found a Philip L. Stevens who graduated in 1995. Is that correct?" she asked.

"No, it would definitely be more recent than that," I said. "I, uh, spilled coffee on part of his form. He either graduated in the last few years, or he's interested in transferring over here to finish his undergrad work and then continue on to grad school."

"I'm sorry," she told me. "There's no more recent student of that name."

I thanked her and hung up.

"Not there?" Joe asked.

"Not there," I replied.

"I bet you know what my next question's going to be," he said.

I nodded. "Where did the money go if it didn't go to pay for Emma and Philip's school expenses?"

• • • •

Joe and I broke into Tess's office for the second time that night. We needed to get a look at her bank account.

But we were having a much harder time hacking into her computer than I'd had with Mr. Davis's.

"Breaking into Tess's wall safe was easier," Joe complained. "And faster."

"If we find out that the money Tess raises for the kids at the Haven ends up in her personal account, we'll have gone a long way toward getting the proof we need," I reminded him.

"We'll definitely have motive," Joe agreed. "She has to have raised millions of dollars over the years. That's the kind of money people kill for." He tried typing in another password. No go. "Hey, it's almost time for people to start waking up," he said.

"I have another idea. Another way we might be able to link Tess to the murders." I hesitated. I thought the plan would work. But it was dangerous.

"Well, what is it? Because what we're doing isn't working," Joe said.

"Here's the thing," I told him. "My idea involves using you as bait."

16.
BAIT

I knocked on Tess's door the next morning. As bait. I was bait. A pink, squirming worm on a hook.

"Come in," Tess called.

I did, and she smiled, like I was the person she most hoped would come walking through the door.

"What can I do for you, Joe?" she asked, waving me to a seat on the sofa in front of her desk.

"I was thinking about what we talked about," I began.

"Now that's something I like to hear," said Tess. She smiled warmly. It was so hard to believe this nice, helpful woman was a killer.

My palms were sweaty, but I didn't want to wipe them against my pants. I didn't want to look nervous. "I went to the library, and I did some reading about lawyers, and what kind of schooling it takes to be one and everything."

She nodded encouragingly, and I rushed on. "It sounds really cool. But I don't think I could get into college. I skipped a lot of high school. It was stupid. I'd just go and hang out at this doughnut place."

"Everybody at the Haven has made mistakes," Tess told me. She reached out and touched my hand. It was hard not to pull away. "Scratch that. *Everybody* has made mistakes. Period. I know I've made some."

Some big ones, I thought. Although I guess you couldn't call theft and murder mistakes exactly.

"I just don't know if I'd be able to pull down the grades to go to college, even if I go to school every single day. No doughnuts. I mean, from what I read, some of the guys who want to be lawyers start at, like, kindergartens for geniuses or something. Then they go to prep school."

"Prep school!" Tess exclaimed. "That's exactly what you need. A couple of years at a good prep school and you'll be in great shape for college."

"Can I even get in?" I asked.

"I'm sure I could work something out," she told me. "First we need to get you the money."

She tapped her lips with one perfectly manicured fingernail. "There's a silent auction being held at a little gallery downtown tonight. The profits are going to the Haven. Why don't you come with me? I'll give a little talk. You can meet everyone; it helps so much to have a face—a young person the possible donors can actually meet. And we'll put all the money from the auction toward prep school for you."

"Really?" I asked.

"Absolutely. Meet me here at my office at eight," Tess told me.

I think she's taken the bait, I thought as I walked out.

"That was awesome!" I exclaimed as I climbed out of the cab after the silent auction.

"It was, wasn't it?" Tess said as she led the way back into the Haven. "I knew you were a good choice. You charmed everyone with that innocent-looking face of yours. The bids on items were ridiculous. One painting went for ten times its actual value. And its actual value was not cheap."

"So how much money do you think I got? Enough for two years of prep school?" I asked.

"Come into my office and let's discuss it," Tess said. I figured this would be a discussion Evan had

had with Tess before he died. Probably even Emma and Philip. And Sean. I thought I might be able to find out where their school money had gone.

When Tess had shut the door behind us, she opened her purse. Then she handed me a one-hundred-dollar bill.

"I don't—why are you giving me this?" I asked.

"You'll get paid every time you work an event with me. That's a pretty good hourly rate, don't you think?" Tess asked.

"Did we not get enough money tonight for school?" I asked. "How many more events will there be?"

"Not all the money will go for school. The bulk of it will go to me, for running the Haven. As I told you, it helps me raise more money if I can put a face on the cause," Tess explained.

"Wait. But you told everyone the money raised would go to my prep school," I protested.

"We'll open a bank account for you," Tess promised. "You can deposit that money tomorrow."

"A hundred dollars? That's all I get?" I jumped to my feet.

"That's all you get for tonight. If you do another event, you'll get another hundred," said Tess. She spoke slowly and clearly, like I was five years old or something.

Sean must have agreed to the hundred-dollars-a-gig deal, I thought. *He must have figured it was better than nothing and that it might even get him to vet school someday.*

"No. Huh-uh. You're not getting away with it." I let my hands curl into fists. I wanted to look furious, the way I was sure Evan and everyone else she had pulled this on had looked.

"I got a lot of business cards tonight," I continued. "A lot of people said I should contact them if I needed a recommendation or anything. I'll call every single person I can and tell them that the money they thought they were giving to me is actually going into your pocket. Don't think I buy that 'it goes to the Haven' bull. I bet you have a nice Swiss bank account that nobody but you knows about."

"I don't plan on discussing any of that with you," said Tess.

"Well, I plan on discussing it with everyone," I yelled. "I'm going to tell everyone about this con you're running." Then a lightbulb went off in my head. Make that a floodlight. I leaned across the desk, getting in her face. "I bet you don't even have a son who ran away," I burst out, remembering her tax forms with no dependents. "I bet you don't have any kind of son at all. That's some sob story you use to get even more cash off of people."

"I admit it. You have me all figured out," Tess said. She didn't sound worried. At all. "But now it's my turn to talk. Sit down," she ordered, her voice ice-cube cold.

"I'm not sitting down," I shouted. "I'm going to go find a phone."

Tess opened the top drawer of her desk and pulled out a folder. "I think you'll want to look at this first." She handed it to me.

It was the folder with the pictures Olivia had taken of me, with me picking that man's pocket. Tess had clearly taken the folder out of the safe because she knew she'd be needing it for this conversation.

"It would be unfortunate if I had to show these pictures to any of the people we met tonight," she said, "or your parents."

"My parents? You have no idea where they are," I retorted.

"No. But I will. I'll have a private investigator get me addresses and phone numbers and even e-mail addresses for both your parents." She smiled. "I bet they'd be relieved to know where their son is."

"This place isn't supposed to contact anyone's parents without permission," I protested.

"That's true. And we don't. At least for most of

the residents. But those teenagers I take a special interest in—sometimes I feel the need to bring their parents into the picture." Tess's smile widened. She thought she had me.

But Frank and I were even closer to having her.

"We need to go to the train station separately," Frank told me the next afternoon. "Tess can't suspect that I'm watching you."

I nodded.

"You're sure she overheard you making that appointment with the reporter?" he asked.

"Yeah. I saw her go into the bathroom. Then I made my call in the alcove nearby and I heard the bathroom door open while I was on the phone," I answered. "I made sure to tell Gwen Anderson that I know what Evan wanted to tell her and that I want to meet and give her the same info."

"Okay. So all we can do is hope she makes a move on you," Frank said.

"Right," I agreed. "All we can do is hope Tess tries to kill me before I get to the reporter—just like she killed Evan."

17.
THANKFUL TO BE ALIVE

I pulled the hood of my sweatshirt low over my face before I started down the stairs to the subway station—the station where Evan had died.

That's not going to happen to Joe, I told myself. *I've got his back*.

As soon as I pushed my way through the turn-stile, I started looking for him. The platform was packed with lunchtime travelers. Where was he? Where was he?

There. I spotted the red T-shirt Joe had bought on the street specially so he'd be easy to see. Now that I'd located him, I started scanning the place for Tess. She had to be here. She wasn't going to let Joe get on the train that would take him to the reporter.

I didn't see her. Something was wrong. Our plan wasn't coming together the way we'd expected it to.

Maybe Tess really hadn't overheard Joe making the phone call to the reporter. Maybe—

I was jerked away from my thoughts by a familiar woman making her way toward Joe from the opposite side of the platform. Not Tess. Olivia. She was a lot closer to Joe than I was.

I crept forward, trying to keep out of Oliva's sight line. Did I have time to circle around behind her?

No. She was picking up her pace. She'd reach him in seconds. And she had a syringe in her hand! She pulled off the orange plastic top as she moved toward Joe.

I broke into a run. I wasn't going to make it. "Joe!" I shouted. "Behind you."

Joe whipped around. Too late. Olivia stabbed the syringe into his throat.

With a roar, I launched myself at Olivia and tackled her to the ground. "What did you give him?" I demanded.

Olivia actually laughed. "You know these street kids. Always overdosing. Tragic."

"Not this time," Joe said. He crouched down next to me and stared at Olivia. "You didn't have time to push the plunger down." He held up the syringe. It was still full.

"You really didn't make a good deal with Tess," I told Olivia. "You take the blackmail pictures for her—and kill when you have to. You've murdered two people at least. And you're still living on the street? You're way underpaid."

"You want to know where I live? I live in a loft in Soho." Olivia struggled to sit up. I pushed down on her shoulders, pinning her to the ground.

"Not for long," Joe told her. "We have evidence against you now." He twirled the syringe between his fingers. "You're going to prison. But maybe it won't be too bad. Maybe you'll be able to share a cell with your friend Tess." He turned to me. "Can you handle this by yourself?" he asked.

"You've got something better to do?" I asked, surprised.

"Did you forget I have an appointment with Gwen Anderson?" Joe reminded me. "I think I have an even better story for her now: a story that all the people who've made donations to the Haven would like to read."

"I'm thankful that my brother has the tackle of an NFL player," Joe announced.

"I'm thankful that my brother can identify a fleur-chon when he sees one," I said.

It was Thanksgiving Day. Everyone around the table was telling the group what they were grateful for.

"Loser, loser, loser," Playback squawked from his perch near the windows.

I turned toward the parrot. "True. Some people would think knowing that much about fashion makes Joe a loser, loser, loser," I said. "But not me."

Joe gave me a kick under the table. I ignored him. Because, as I always say, sometimes that's all you can do with Joe.

"I'm thankful for second chances," Mrs. Fowler contributed, looking at Lily, who was sitting across from her.

Lily wasn't living at home. But she was going to family therapy with her parents—both of them. And my mom had helped hook her up with a great foster family. Give my mother a problem and a computer and she'll come up with a solution in minutes. It's a research librarian thing.

"I'm thankful I have sons who make the world a better place," Dad stated.

"Better, maybe. But not cleaner," said Aunt Trudy. "Have you seen the stain on Frank's coat? I haven't even been able to figure out what it is, which makes me thankful for new, improved Stain Away."

Mom looked around the table. "I'm thankful for friends—old and new. And I'm thankful to have my whole family here at home."